COLUMBUS

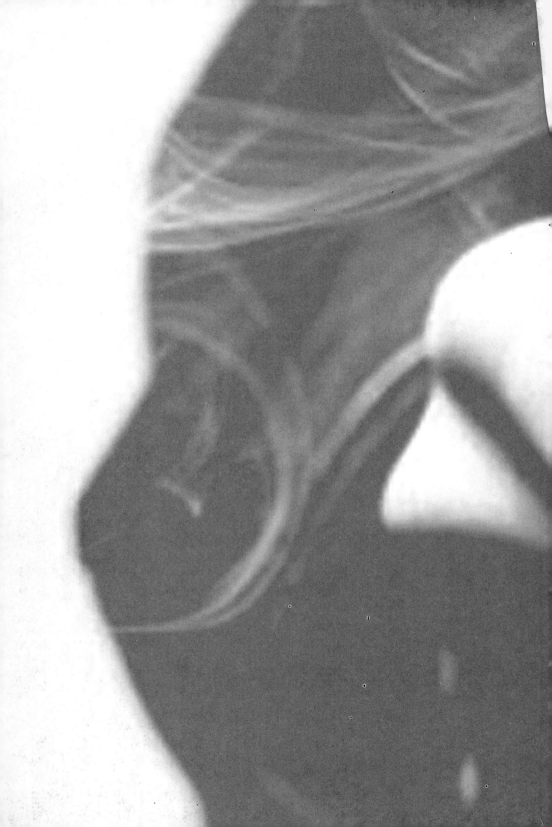

COLUMBUS

DEREK HAAS

PEGASUS BOOKS
NEW YORK

COLUMBUS

Pegasus Books LLC

80 Broad Street, Fifth Floor

New York, NY 10004

Copyright © 2009 by Derek Haas

First Pegasus Books edition 2009

Library of Congress Cataloging-in-Publication Data is available.

Designed by Lorie Pagnozzi

ISBN: 978-1-60598-068-3

10 9 8 7 6 5 4 3 2 1

Printed in the United States of America
Distributed by W. W. Norton & Company, Inc.
www.pegasusbooks.us

FOR MICHAEL, WHO DIRECTED.
AND FOR MOLLY, WHO PRODUCED.

COLUMBUS

CHAPTER ONE

IF YOU'RE ASKING ME TO LOOK BACK ON MY LIFE AND FIND ANSWERS TO YOUR QUESTIONS, OR IF YOU'RE HOPING FOR AN EXPLANATION OR AN APOLOGY FOR MY ACTIONS, YOU ARE GOING TO BE DISAPPOINTED. I have not softened. I have not changed. Once I commit to killing a target, death follows.

I told you not to like me.

It is overcast in Rome. A wall of gray clouds have rolled in and settled over the city like a conquering army. Shop owners and businessmen cast upward glances, trying to gauge whether or not rain is inevitable. They think maybe the sky is just posturing, threatening, but they unpack their umbrellas just the same.

I am dressed in the dark slacks and long-sleeve sweaters commonly worn by locals this time of year. My Italian has steadily improved, though my accent will never be without flaw. I had hoped to master the inflections, to be able to pass myself off as a native, but my speech pattern lacks authenticity, and I am easily pegged as an English speaker within a few short sentences. This has hampered my ability to blend in, which I've always worn like a protective coat in the States. As such, I have learned to say as little as possible.

I make my way up a street named the *Largo Delle Sette Chiese*, and head for a small restaurant crammed to the breaking point with tables and customers and food and waiters too busy to give a damn about smiling. The menu is authentic Roman, as is the customer service; servers drop off plates and silverware and expect patrons to set the table for themselves. Most tourists aren't smart enough to frequent the place, the *Ar Grottino der Traslocatore*, preferring the homier pasta and fish shops around the Spanish Steps or near the Colosseum.

I drop into a wooden chair across from my fence, my middleman, an astute, stoic businessman named William Ryan. He has been my fence for a couple of years now, and though we relocated to Europe together following an assignment where my old fence was gunned down and I killed my father with my bare hands, our relationship remains strictly a business one.

"How was your flight?"

"Mercifully short."

Ryan had bought a home in Paris in the expensive Eighth arrondissement, above an art gallery near the Bristol Hotel. We meet in Rome whenever he wants to hand me a new assignment. Files are only passed in person, never mailed. I have asked him to move to Italy, but he prefers the amenities of Parisian living.

"I trust you're ready to go back to work, Columbus?"

It has been two months since my last assignment, the execution of a corrupt Belgian police superintendent in Brussels. He had been a vain man who thought himself untouchable up until the moment I touched him.

A waiter breaks off to take our order and soon fills the table with *straccetti alla rucola* and *bistecca di lombo*.

"Yes. As soon as possible."

I can only take off a couple of months before I get restless, itchy. Anything more and I feel my edge slipping. Once the edge dulls, it can take drastic measures to sharpen it.

Ryan extracts a thick manila envelope from a leather satchel. To anyone watching, we are simply businessmen conducting business in the bustle of a packed Italian restaurant. It is too noisy for other customers to hear our conversation, though we would never discuss anything suspicious in public.

I transfer the envelope to my lap, and it feels like a brick has been placed there, solid and heavy. An image pops into my head, a man being crushed to death under stones while groaning "more weight" through clenched teeth. Where is that from? Something I read a long time ago, perhaps when I was incarcerated at a juvenile detention center named Waxham in western Massachusetts. I was sent there, along with my only friend, for killing one of our foster parents after suffering years of brutality. That place was responsible for my education in more ways than one, a rung on the ladder to where I stand now.

Ryan picks over his food. "The client pays a premium."

"Where do you gauge the level of difficulty?"

"Medium."

I nod, absorbing this.

We finish our meal without talking, and when the waiter clears the table and takes Ryan's cash, we stand and shake hands.

"The job is in Prague. If you need anything additional from me, don't hesitate."

"Thank you."

"The logistics are covered in the file. Take care, Columbus."

"You too."

We head away in opposite directions.

The name at the top of the page is Jiri Dolezal. His file indicates he is a Czech banker, a man whose hands are buried up to the wrists in drug rings and prostitution rings and pornography rings and anything else illicit into which he can force his way. He is a bad egg, and it is obvious if he is suddenly discovered with his shell cracked, the Czech police will sniff around just long enough to look like they give a shit before labeling the case "unsolved."

Ryan's file on the subject is thick and thorough. My former fence, Pooley, excelled at putting these files together, documenting as many facts about the target as possible and compiling them into a dossier to give me a detailed glimpse into a mark's life. But Ryan is a true master craftsman, I have to admit; his work in this area—the depth of information he uncovers—is extraordinary, uncanny, far surpassing even Pooley's best efforts.

The pages inside the file serve two purposes. The first is practical: I need to look for the best place to strike the target and make my subsequent escape. Any piece of information might help. The route the target takes to work. The restaurants he frequents. The blueprints of his house, his office. Even personal information like the names of his children or his nieces and nephews or his dying father can feasibly come into play, can put the target at ease, can get me invited into his house or his office where I can shoot him without impediment. The more information Ryan provides, the less I have to rely on dangerous improvisation.

The second purpose the file serves is psychological. It is difficult to explain, but the job I do—the professional killing of men—exacts a mental toll. The only way to diminish this toll is to make a connection with the target, to find some evil in the mark and exploit that evil in my mind. An olive-skinned Italian man named Vespucci explained this to me a lifetime ago in a small apartment in Boston when I first walked this path. He said that I must *make* the connection so I can *sever* the connection. He said he could not explain why it was so, just that it was. I heard from Ryan that Vespucci had died recently, though I didn't hear how. I wonder if that old man went down swinging, or if he was finally crushed beneath the weight of his personal stones.

Still, there is one incongruous nugget in Dolezal's file. **Mark frequents a rare bookstore in Prague located on Valentinska. He collects Izaak Walton and Horace Walpole.**

The information seems odd to me, like a flower emerging through the crack of a sidewalk. Nothing else in the dossier suggests Dolezal is more than a humorless thug. His life seems regimented, colorless; and yet, here is something unconventional. A collection indicates a passion. So why rare books, and why these authors in particular? Make the connection. I need to make the connection, get inside the target's head, so I can sever the connection.

I enter a tiny shop in Rome on the Via Poli named Zodelli. The cramped room is lined with shelves, all holding leather-bound books behind glass enclosures. The bulbs are dim, and it takes my eyes a moment to adjust to the absence of light. A gray-haired woman sits behind a desk, marking a ledger with a pencil. I greet her in Italian and she looks up and smiles perfunctorily, then calls out "Risina!"

I turn to better examine the nearest row of books and wait with my hands stuffed in my pockets. The shelf appears to hold several volumes of the same book, *The Life and Letters of Charles Dickens*, bound in red. From what I can see, the covers look as fresh and spotless as new pieces of furniture.

"These are first editions from 1872..."

There are two facets to a woman's beauty. The first is internal, the beauty found in the kindness of eyes, in a simple gesture, in a soft voice. The second is physical, the kind that strikes you like a punch in the stomach and threatens to take your breath away, to suffocate you. The woman standing next to me is stunning. She's wearing a simple black dress, and her dark hair is tied up, but one strand has fallen away and passes over an eye to gently kiss her cheek.

And yet there is something else in her face. An undercurrent I've spotted on a few of my marks. What is it? Sadness? Loneliness? Whatever it is, it only serves to join the two facets together, like a peg bolting inside a lock.

"Here, take a look." She unlocks the glass partition and withdraws one of the books from the shelf. I have to concentrate to pull my eyes from her in order to focus on the book. "You see? It's a beautiful series. It has twelve Cosway-style portraits depicting Dickens over the course of his life. Amazing. Octavo, see, with raised bands, green gilt inlays on the front panels, gilt doblures, watered silk endpapers . . . yes? Really magnificent. Perfect condition."

I find my voice. "Your English is quite good."

She smiles. "I went to university in America."

"Which part?"

"Boston."

"I know the city."

"I loved it there. But Italy called. Italy always calls when you leave her. It is difficult not to answer."

I hand her the book back and she looks at it one more time like she's studying the photograph of an old classmate before returning it to the shelf.

"Now, Mr. Walker, how can I help you?"

I had done some digging the last few days and, through a series of phone calls and references, made an appointment using a fake name at Zodelli with a Risina Lorenzana. My plan was to get inside my mark's head, understand his fascination with rare books, feel how he must feel as he tracks down and purchases an old manuscript. I don't speak Czech and didn't want to draw attention to myself by using the same bookstore as my mark, so I chose one near to me. I had been expecting a bookish elderly woman with a haughty manner like the one sitting behind the desk to wait on me. Not this. Not her.

"I'll confess I'm a dabbler. I have only a little experience in collecting rare books."

"Do you like literature?"

"Very much."

"Then you are no dabbler. You have already started collecting. Up here." She smiles and taps her index finger to her temple.

"Are you familiar with Izaak Walton?"

"*The Compleat Angler*, yes? A wonderful book to collect . . . do you like to fish?"

"I like to catch things."

Her smile widens, the kind that starts in her eyes before spreading to her mouth and cheeks. That underlying current fades a bit.

"I do too. I think it is innate, this feeling." She touches my forearm as she says this, a chuckle in her voice. Even after she moves to the desk, pulls out a binder and flips through it, I can still feel her fingers on my skin.

She shakes her head, turning a page. "I'm afraid I do not have any Walton on hand, but it is . . . um . . . not much effort to find one for you."

"Is that how it works? Collectors come to you to find specific books for them?"

"Yes, that is part of the job, yes. Also, I hunt for books coming on the market . . . auctions, estate sales, through a . . . what's the American word . . . network? I have friends and contacts at other shops who let me know when something interesting is up for sale. A network, yes?"

"And rivals?"

"Yes . . . it can be competitive. But it is as you say, I like to catch things."

Her whole face lights up when she says this, and there is something familiar about the expression. I think I've worn it myself a few times.

"How long would it take you to locate one for me?"

"First edition?"

"Yes."

"I will have to call a few people, but I do not think long. As old as the book is, it was very popular in its time. There are quite a few on the market. I should be able to find it for a fair price. How may I contact you?"

I write down an e-mail address for her, and she hands me her card. "You can reach me any time . . . that is my personal mobile number."

"I look forward to hearing from you."

"I'll start fishing," she says with a laugh as I head for the door.

It will be a while before the image of her face leaves my head. And that undercurrent, that emotion she tries to bite down but can't quite pull off, is as intriguing to me as a wrapped box. I need to know more about Risina Lorenzana; I have to know more.

These are thoughts I should not be having.

Darkness descends on Prague quickly, like someone tossed a blanket over the sun. The city at night is quiet and expectant, the cold of winter chasing most tourists to warmer hemispheres. It is foot-stamping weather, and icicles hang like incisors from the buildings of Old Town. The moon hides, as though afraid of what's coming.

I am in my third week of tracking Jiri Dolezal, making the connection so I can sever the connection. It is easy to blend in here . . . thick, bulky coats, dark toboggans for the head, and full beards conspire to make all men look uniform. In the winter, it is simply too cold to pick out a stranger on the street, or to notice a professional killer as he stalks his prey.

I am in a basement restaurant near the St. Charles Bridge, an authentic Czech establishment serving duck, rabbit, lamb, and potatoes in a large pot brought right to the table. As beautiful as the city is—the bridge itself is a marvel of medieval craftsmanship—the insides of the traditional restaurants are mausoleums: dark, cramped, and smoky. I have my head buried in a book while my fork moves regularly from dish to mouth. I don't say much, don't move much, just blend into the wall like a piece of old furniture.

Two men sit in a dark corner, smoking Petras and drinking vodka. They run a nightclub for Dolezal, an ostentatious techno-dance hall that specializes in transporting women from the brothels outside of town to a less threatening location for tourists.

Ryan's file indicates that these men, Bedrich Novotny and Dusan Chalupnik, have been skimming money from the boss, bumping liquor prices on cash sales and ringing up only half the purchases while pocketing the rest. They also have deals with the working girls to pad their prices and split the profits, unbeknownst to their employer. It is a tightrope walk, this scamming of a scammer, and these men are either too reckless or too stupid to pull it off successfully.

They have been summoned to meet Dolezal tonight, and it is obvious from the way they pick at their food and tap their legs up and down continuously, they suspect the old man might have caught wind of their play. Though I can't speak their language, I gather they are comparing notes tonight, getting their stories straight before meeting the man they are defrauding.

It is one thing to read about a mark's misdeeds in a dossier, although Ryan does an amazing job of chronicling them explicitly. It is quite another to experience them first hand, to witness evil in a man up close, to see his face as he metes out punishment. I have learned over the years that perhaps the best way to get to know a mark is to watch his employees, to see how they carry themselves, witness for myself how they are treated. When looking for evil to exploit, watch the men right below the man. They are his representatives, a part of the mark himself.

After an hour, Novotny and Chalupnik don their coats and shuffle out into the night. I settle my bill and follow discreetly. Prague is a walking city for many of the residents, and these men are no exception. They certainly aren't worried about being tracked; they're both wearing bright red parkas and smoking cigarettes like they're determined to reach the bottom of the pack. They mumble to each other as they go, and though I don't understand the words, I can pick up the tightness of their speech, like their windpipes are constricting as they get closer to the meeting point.

They arrive at a corner where Partyzanska Street meets a set of railroad tracks and stand under a lamppost, their backs to me, waiting. My eyes have long since adjusted to the darkness, and it is easy for me to watch those red parkas from a stoop a block away. I am invisible here; even my frozen breath I've learned to trap in my black scarf by breathing slowly out of the side of my mouth.

Fifteen minutes pass and they check their watches. Their voices reach me over the wind, irritated, frustrated. If they were planning on coming here to make an angry stand, the delay has taken the wind from their sails. Just as a freight train approaches, rounding the corner, I see a large man approaching them from behind rapidly, pulling a handgun from the small of his back.

Gunfire erupts, two shots, the report of a low-caliber pistol, pop, pop, barely audible over the thunder of the train. The two men pitch forward, their foreheads opening, and crash to the sooty pavement, side by side, their limbs splayed out at absurd angles. The train passes and the shooter retreats down the adjacent alley to my right until I can no longer see him or hear his footsteps.

I wait twenty minutes, though I'm sure the killer is long gone, and then head back the way I came. I've seen all I need to see.

At Waxham Juvenile Hall, boys learned all the ways of dirty fighting, but nothing was held in more contempt and less respect than the sucker punch. Decking someone from behind with a fist to the temple, or shoving a pencil into someone's back was considered the lowest of the low, and any kid who pulled that shit soon found himself friendless, alone, vulnerable.

Jiri Dolezal took care of business by sucker-punching his men, gunning them down when they couldn't see it or hear it coming. I'm not sure if he pulled the trigger, or simply ordered it done, but I had little doubt it was his decision, his play, and it gave me all I needed to plan his death.

I return to Rome for one purpose, to pick up a first-edition copy of Izaak Walton's *The Compleat Angler*. There are a hundred ways I could have paid for the book and had it delivered to me without setting foot inside Zodelli's, but I find my feet moving through the door like they are operating on their own, no mind to guide them, enchanted.

"Mr. Walker!" Risina greets me warmly, and now it is my throat constricting.

"Good afternoon," I manage.

"Just give me one moment. I have your book in the back."

She heads through a swinging wooden door, leaving me alone in the shop. The truth is, I don't need to be here. I've done what I set out to do, to get inside the mind of my target, and the rare-book world is a dead end, a pointless triviality, with no evil to exploit. So why am I here? Why did I travel all the way back to Rome? Why am I waiting to look into a face flawlessly exhibiting both kinds of beauty? Because there's an undercurrent in her face I need to explore.

"Ahh, here it is. Have a look?"

I take the volume in my hand, and study the front . . . the author's name in white text above the black title of the book, and then an illustration of a pair of men nestled under a tree, casting lines into a river.

"Remarkable condition for a seventeenth-century novel, yes?"

I nod. "It's amazing."

"I will admit I read through it while I was waiting for you to pick it up. I studied literature in school, yes, but my seventeenth-century experience is limited. Milton, yes, some of the poets like Herbert, Donne . . . but Walton passed me by. You have inspired me."

"I'll confess I know nothing about him. I told a friend I might start collecting books, and he suggested this one. But now I feel like I shouldn't touch it, just put it on a shelf. . . ."

She makes a clucking sound with her mouth, like a schoolteacher correcting a student. "No, no, no, Mr. Walker. Hang paintings on a wall, put photographs on a shelf, but books . . . no, they are alive. They are meant to be handled. Open the pages and read them. Only then are they worth collecting, once you know what's inside."

I smile at her and Risina returns it, and there's that underlying hint of sadness there, like the bass note of a perfume. The corners of her mouth turn up, but only slightly. I feel a spot opening up in my stomach, like someone has hooked a line there and is towing me toward her. Goddamn, do I need to know more about her. But to what end? What can it possibly gain me but complications in a life where it remains essential I be alone?

After I pay for the book, she offers her hand. "Please come back to see me, Mr. Walker. We can start to grow your collection."

"I would like that," I say, and since there is no other practical reason for me to remain, I head for the door. This will be the last time I see her, I lie to myself, and take one last look at her behind the desk as I head out into the street.

Jiri Dolezal will die tonight. He is in his office, working late, surrounded by a skeletal staff: an assistant, a bodyguard, and his cousin, who oversees his ledgers. Dolezal didn't luck into his fortune; he worked extremely hard at the business of evil. His work ethic would almost be admirable if he applied it toward say, fighting world poverty instead of exploiting teenage girls in the Eastern European sex trade.

Ninety-nine times out of a hundred, I do not know who hires me. Our fences are designed as a barrier between assassin and client, to protect us from each other. It is better this way. I don't need to know the motivation for why someone placed a hit on my mark. I only need to validate the inherent evil in my target so I can make my kill and walk away.

Occasionally, though, I discover the client in the course of the hunt. The file will hint at a possibility, and if beneficial, I can use that information to assist me. I just have to be right.

I break into the building using the oldest of techniques: a tension wrench and a steel lockpick. While Prague has made great strides toward joining the new century, security is surprisingly Old World. It is as though the new crop of organized criminals believes the fear and intimidation popularized by the old government regime is enough to keep danger at bay.

I march to the second-floor office and knock on the door, brazenly. I can hear everything go quiet in the room, like I've caught its occupants in some nefarious act, and then a man with a baritone voice barks an order to someone nearer to my position.

The door swings open and the secretary fills the space. She measures me with a dour expression. She says something in Czech, and I respond by holding up the book Risina tracked down for me. With my best British accent, I say, "I understand Mr. Dolezal collects Izaak Walton."

She frowns and clucks over her shoulder. After a brief argument from which I can guess the gist, the door opens further, and I step into the room.

Dolezal is behind his desk, ten feet away. He has a fat face and a nose that lists to the left, like it was broken and never reset. To my right is the cousin, who barely looks up from his laptop. The bodyguard, who is easily a head taller than me, stands next to him. I am confident he is the man who pulled the trigger on Novotny and Chalupnik, the one who shot them at close range from behind.

In my left hand, I hold the first edition *Compleat Angler*. It is like a magician's feint . . . it draws the eye to it and away from my free hand. The bodyguard steps in to frisk me, which is always a good time to strike. When the big man is stooped over, his hands on my waist instead of his weapon, he is vulnerable.

He starts to pat me down and my right hand finds that pistol he keeps in the small of his back. I have it out of his waistband and up in the blink of an eye. It's a double-action, nine millimeter Czech CZ-TT, a little small for me but it will do just fine in close quarters. Dolezal is still staring at the book in my left hand when the bullet shatters that misshapen nose of his for good. I hit him square, a sucker punch he never saw coming.

The loud report of the gun is like an electric shock to the bodyguard. He leaps backward, takes one look at his boss, and his face falls. I can see the calculations working out in his mind, can see his brain forming the wrong decision. The secretary starts to bellow like a siren but I'm not worried about her. The bodyguard sets his legs to pounce, lowers his head to charge me—if he's going down, he's going down a fighter even though the battle is already decided.

Just as I swing the gun around, the cousin rises up behind him, wielding that laptop like a mallet. He brings it down with everything he has on top of the bodyguard's head. The big man drops like someone kicked his legs out from under him as the laptop cracks across the back of his head, shattering into a hundred pieces.

The cousin gives me a satisfied look but I keep my face neutral, drop the pistol next to the capsized guard, and hurry toward the stairwell. I was hoping I wasn't going to have to kill the bodyguard. In my experience, killing anyone other than the target creates a mess. So I let the forgotten man in the room take care of him, the cousin, the one who hired me. Since I don't know where the secretary's loyalties lie, I am gone before she can make a decision. If she had planned it with the cousin, had been a part of hiring me, I'll never know.

I know exactly what I'm doing, goddammit. I'm clearing my mind, recharging my batteries, wiping my slate clean so I will be fresh for a new assignment. I am getting my mind right.

So why am I once again in Rome, sitting in a small *trattoria* near the Trevi fountain?

"I hate it, actually," Risina is saying. "My sister was six or seven when my mother was pregnant, carrying me. For some inexplicable reason, my mother asked her to name me. She was so young, and I suppose was playing off of the common name Rosina, which means 'rose,' and instead came up with Risina, which means nothing except that I have had to correct people all my life."

"I would say 'a rose by any other name' but I'm sure you've heard that before."

She smiles genuinely. "Only once or twice."

The last fifteen years have taught me many things, but above all else is this: I cannot do what I do and maintain a relationship. There are no rules in the assassination world, no code, no honor amongst thieves. There are no civilians, no untouchable targets. If I continue to escalate this, if I continue to see Risina, then I have thrust her into this game despite the fact she will not know she's playing. I have pounded my head against this immovable wall twice before. With Pooley, who died, and with a girl I loved, Jake Owens, whom I had to forcibly remove from my life. I thought I could go back to her, but I was wrong.

So what am I doing here? Jiri Dolezal is dead; my connection to the rare-book world has been severed. So why do I keep returning to that bookstore on the Via Poli, why am I still pretending to be a collector, why did I hire Risina to track down another *Compleat Angler* for me? Why did I suggest dinner tonight?

Is it because I'm searching for some vestige of humanity in myself and I'm willing to put another life in danger, if only to satisfy my basest instincts?

I'll say it again. I told you not to like me.

CHAPTER TWO

THE MARK'S NAME IS ANTON NOEL. He is the fifty-two-year-old chief information officer of a French pharmaceutical company based in Paris named Ventus-Safori. He has worked there for over two decades, rising through the ranks since he was hired out of school as an assistant accountant in the late eighties. The attached surveillance photos reveal a man who has not passed on too many crepes since graduation.

Ryan and I met outside a cathedral in Turin to exchange the file.

"It's the same procurer as the Prague job."

"That's the fourth time they've hired me."

"They like your work."

"I met the fence...."

"Doriot."

"Yes. I met him in Brussels before the first job when he wanted to take a look at me. He was hard to read."

Ryan looked at me with a level expression. "Which means he's a professional."

"Yeah. I get that. He's still the one handling affairs for this client, then?"

Ryan nodded.

"I don't want to get too tied to one contractor. I mean, I think we should—"

My fence held up one palm as though nothing further needed to be said on the subject. "I understand. You still want this file then, or do you want me to beg off to Doriot?"

"No, I'll take it."

He handed it to me, and I felt that weight again. Heavier this time. The stones piling up.

Ryan stared hard at me. "You sure you're ready, Columbus?"

"Of course."

He looked like he had something more to say, but I avoided his eyes. Finally, we shook hands and left.

Now, with the file in my hand, I pore over its contents, an uneasy feeling prickling my brain. *Am* I ready? What did Ryan see in me that made him ask that question?

Noel appears to be a typical rich European businessman. He

keeps a mistress in a small apartment on the Left Bank. He employs a couple of Serbian bodyguards, veterans from a mostly forgotten war. He travels a few times a month by private jet to London or New York or Geneva. Peculiarly, he drives his own car, a Mercedes, and has his bodyguards sit behind him and in the passenger seat. This piques my interest, the way Dolezal's rare-book collection stood out on the page for me. If he's chauffeuring his bodyguards around, then he isn't particularly concerned with his own protection. Or he's arrogant, controlling, a trait I've seen in some of these business titans. They don't want to relinquish control of any part of their lives, even the mundane.

Possibilities emerge in front of me. Take him en route to work, while he's behind the wheel? Take him at the private airfield housing his jet? Strike when he's occupied with his mistress? Take that control he cherishes and turn it against him?

I should have left for Paris already. I am four weeks into an eight-week assignment and I should be following my mark, forming strike plans, identifying his weaknesses, searching for evil.

But I am with Risina, in her small apartment in Rome, keeping that weight off me, even if the relief is only temporary.

Her cooking is awful. The pasta is chewy, the sauce is bland, the cheese on top is strong enough to melt my nose, and I love every bite of it. A home-cooked anything is enticing for someone who barely knows the meaning of the word "home," and if the wine has to flow to wash it down, so be it.

She looks at me across the table, her fork poised in midair.

"I seem to talk a great bit about myself, and when I leave you, I realize I've learned nothing new about you."

"I find you interesting."

She points the fork at me. "I know what you're doing and it won't work."

"What am I doing?"

"I am going to ask you a direct question and you are going to turn it around back to me."

"Ask."

"Okay. I will ask this. What do you do for a living that brings you to Italia so often?"

"That's an easy one. Why did you start working with book collectors?"

She laughs and wags her finger. "I told you."

There are two parts to lying, and both require practice. One is to hold your eyes steady and to speak with only a hint of inflection. The second is to make the lie so plain and uninteresting as to rule out any follow-up questions.

I set my face. "My work is boring. I work for an airline company. I buy and sell parts for airplane wings. I line up contracts all over the world."

"You see. That is not boring. You are an international business-man."

"A boring international businessman."

"But as you say, you travel all over the world."

"Doing a job any man can do."

"I think you are modest."

"Just telling the truth."

And the corners of her mouth turn up into a smile, this one stretching farther, because she is with a man who tells the truth, who is safe, who is humble about his life. The sadness below the surface has dissipated, at least a bit.

She takes a bite of her pasta and makes a face.

"My cooking is terrible."

"No," I say and keep my gaze locked. "I mean, I can't feel my tongue any more, but it's really wonderful."

She erupts in laughter, the infectious kind, color coming to her cheeks.

"Okay, we're going to try something only one time," she says as she pushes her plate to the center of the table, dismissing it.

"What?"

"We're going to ask each other one question and no topic is how-do-you-say. . . ."

"Off limits?"

"Yes, taboo. Off limits. And the other has to answer truthfully, no matter what is asked. Maybe we'll learn something and want to learn more, or maybe after hearing the answer, we'll decide we just aren't . . . we just don't want to keep seeing each other."

"Sounds dangerous."

"Possibly."

"Okay, I'm in."

"Okay?"

I nod and she smiles.

"Can I ask first?"

I nod again.

"Why do you want to see me, Jack?"

I don't have to set my face, don't have to lie, not this time. "I want to know who put that sadness in your eyes, in your cheeks."

She leans back, the answer catching her off guard, and folds her arms across her chest. For a long moment, she doesn't say anything, and even the air in the room seems to still.

"Is that your question to me?"

"That's my answer to your question. I haven't asked one yet."

She nods, forces a smile. Her voice stays low. "Okay, then, what is your question?"

"We don't have to—"

"Don't be silly. This was my idea."

"Okay. Are you ready?"

She lowers her eyes like she's bracing herself, and her nod is barely perceptible.

I wait until she looks up, then arrest her eyes with mine. "My question is this. What is the recipe for this pasta?"

She blinks, and then starts laughing again. It is a sound that will stay with me for the next few weeks, holding me afloat like a life preserver.

The signs are there, if you pay attention. Little things: you bang your shin into the coffee table in the morning, or you step off a curb into a puddle of sewer water, or you can't find your wallet, your keys, your jacket, no matter how hard you look. Bad luck has a way of building momentum, of summoning its strength like an ocean wave before crashing down over you, knocking you off your feet. If you can spot the signs, you might be fortunate enough not to drown.

Paris is chilly and gray in February, though it is desperately trying to maintain its charm. There is something sad about it, like a hostess doing her best to keep a party together after the first guests start trickling away. Stores and restaurants are open, but outside tables are empty and silent. People shuffle by without talking, hurrying to get where they're going, lighting cigarettes without breaking stride.

I have seen Anton Noel four times. Once, at a charity auction where I monitored him from a crowd inside an art gallery. Once, at a business conference where he droned on in French about the necessity of product diversification in emerging global markets. And twice, I have watched him driving his Mercedes, heading out of the gate where the Rue du St. Paul meets the Rue St. Antoine.

The gate is well guarded, with two dark-suited men perking up whenever the boss is about to roll outside, and a bevy of cameras pointing out at the street. I can watch the gate from the front window of a café a block away without drawing attention to myself . . . just order a coffee and a pastry while I pretend to read an American newspaper. The guards are a signal; they sit relaxed throughout most of the day, slumped in stiff chairs, even when a delivery truck or visitor crosses through the gates. However, when a white phone near the gate rings, they both rise to attention and stand erect, eyes sweeping the area, always five minutes before the black Mercedes drives out, Noel at the wheel, his bodyguards in the passenger seat and behind him.

Most often, it is this type of security I find myself up against: lax, poorly conceived, untrained. These guards—and the ones riding in the Mercedes—are simply window-dressing, as empty and impotent as a scarecrow in a field. They work as a deterrent against amateur thieves and muggers and kidnappers, but are worthless against a professional contract killer.

And herein lies the rub: it is my duty, my obligation, to keep my concentration at the highest level, to eliminate my prey flawlessly, even when faced with unworthy opposition. This is how I became what the Russians call a Silver Bear, an assassin who commands top fees because he never defaults on a job. I became one by never underestimating my mark, by treating every job as if it were my last.

"Your espresso."

"*Merci.*"

The shop owner has shuffled over carrying a saucer and a small cup and I keep my face pleasant and unmemorable.

"This weather . . . pfff," he says and I just want him to hand me my drink and move back to the counter. I've learned not to start up conversations, not to engage with Europeans who spot an English-speaker and want to practice the language. There is a way of holding my face still, of acting like I am deep in thought, concentrating on the paper, that makes waiters or shop owners leave the food behind and walk away without thinking further of it, without thinking "I should remember this asshole. I better keep an eye on him."

My behavior is working, the man is already whispering *perdons* as he sets down the saucer, is already taking one step backward, but he didn't place the saucer carefully on the railing and the plate and cup topple over, spilling espresso all over my pants before crashing to the floor.

He starts cursing himself in French, all apologies and wishes for forgiveness and how could he be such an oaf, and I just tell him not to worry about it, it's cool, don't worry at all, but now others are looking at me in the shop and my anonymity is slightly compromised.

Bad luck. You can remain focused, hone your concentration, but you are powerless against luck when it sours and turns against you. I cannot allow it to build, so I am up and moving out the door, leaving five euros behind which should be enough to make him happy his error didn't cost him my business.

I am going to kill Noel today. I am going to kill him on this street, when I see the guards receive the phone call and the black Mercedes pull out of the gate and turn in this direction, toward the end of the narrow lane. I am going to be seated on an old Honda motorcycle, idling on the left side of the road. When he drives past me I am going to shoot him in the face through his driver's side window. The car will be moving when I shoot him, which will cause the vehicle to continue forward into a row of parked cars, so that by the time his bodyguards and any on-lookers realize what is happening, I will be ten blocks away.

I was planning on having five minutes after I hear the white phone ring to quietly pay for my drink and head out, still reading my newspaper, and then I would sit on top of the motorcycle, folding the paper back, appearing like I'm finishing an article while my right hand slips inside my jacket and finds my Glock. But now that plan has to be modified.

I can't loiter at the end of the street, can't draw any suspicion to myself. The time Noel leaves varies each afternoon; the only clue is the white phone ringing.

I should abort, should do this job tomorrow, but I hesitated too long in Rome, didn't get started on my surveillance until the sixth week on this job and the contractor is expecting a dead body by the time the sun sets tonight. I have put all my eggs in the white phone basket. My two previous scouts proved it would be an effective strategy, a way to exploit his flawed sense of security.

I can't go back to square one anyway; the café owner would remember me now. If I entered his shop tomorrow at the same time, he would have another reason to recognize my face and make contact and continue to apologize and my anonymity would be surrendered completely. It has to be today.

I deserve this bad luck because I am mentally unprepared. Risina. Even now my thoughts are drifting to the last conversation we had, seated in the train station in Rome, her hair pulled back in a tight ponytail.

"There is something about you, Jack, between the words that you say."

"You're making me sound more interesting than I am. . . ." I had a hard time looking away from her. I am a man who is always checking angles, noting the body language of strangers in my periphery. And yet my eyes continued to lock on hers like she was the only one in the station.

"For someone who loves books as much as I do, I'm terrible at reading people. But with you, I feel like there's a missing chapter. Someone maybe ripped it free and you're reluctant to put it back."

"Who told you you were bad at reading people?"

"I know I am, Jack. I've had very few . . . I've gotten to know very few people."

"Well, I'm glad you want to get to know me."

"I do. I want to know—"

The white phone is ringing, snapping me back to the present. My luck isn't so bad after all, I am halfway to the small Honda motorcycle and I no longer have to come up with a plan to loiter and watch the street. Anton Noel has unwittingly sealed his fate by simply leaving his office early. It didn't take me long after I landed in Paris to find evil in the man to exploit. I learned through Ryan that his company, Ventus-Safori, is famous for rushing experimental drugs to market, for paying off France's government drug administration to ensure their pills are first on pharmacy shelves. This has resulted in three recalls since Noel rose to power, twice after the deaths of more than a dozen adults due to heart complications from hastily manufactured cholesterol blockers. And once, following the deaths of three infants from a cold medicine that should never have been allowed on the market. Internal memos revealed all three were known to be risky, but bribes in the right places assured millions of Euros were made before the company's troubled medications could be removed from store counters. All lawsuits were fought vigorously, and the company's stock price withstood the bad press. I had little doubt Anton Noel had carefully factored in the risks and was more concerned with profits than with his customers' health. Or lack thereof.

The black Mercedes is emerging from the gate as the two guards stand sentinel on either side, providing their hapless guise of security.

I am seated on the motorcycle as planned, my right hand gripping the handle of the automatic pistol. In the rectangle of my sideview mirror, I can see the car turning my way and heading up the street. Just a few more seconds and Noel will be dead and the spilled coffee on my pants will just be a nuisance instead of a premonition of more bad luck to come and I can head back to Rome to see that smile on Risina's face and that one strand of hair kissing her cheek and the car pulls up alongside me, about to pass. My gun is out and up and only then do I realize Noel is not behind the wheel but riding in the passenger seat.

The file said he always drove. Always. My two previous visits to the Rue St. Antoine confirmed the veracity of this statement, and my strategy was conceived to exploit it. So why this fucking day? Why right now of all times in the year for him to let his bodyguard drive and he is hunched over a BlackBerry in the passenger seat, punching in God knows what and his bodyguard's eyes go wide as he spots my pistol just a foot from his window and the wave of bad luck rolls over my head and my second of hesitation is enough.

The guard jams on the accelerator like he's trying to kick his heel through the floorboard and the Mercedes jumps like a whipped horse just as I register what is happening and fire my pistol. I only catch the bodyguard's shoulder through the window, but it might be enough. On any other day, it would probably be enough.

Instead of crashing, the Mercedes is tearing down the Rue St. Antoine, clipping the sides of parked vehicles as my thumb hits the ignition and I straddle the Honda while one hand holds my Glock and I gun the motorcycle after the fleeing sedan.

I allowed this to happen, hell I *caused* this to happen because I took this job lightly. I blinked, I stayed in Rome when I should have been here dissecting an infinite number of preferable ways to kill this target instead of cavalierly choosing *this* way, this ridiculously flawed, inept way.

No more. I set my jaw and drop my eyes into slits and pin down the throttle while the heel of my boot hovers over the back brake like a wild ram steeling itself for an attack. I am Columbus, I am a Silver Bear, and when Anton Noel leaves that Mercedes it will be at the hands of a coroner.

Ahead, the sedan whips into a hard right down a one-way commercial street in the middle of the Jewish quarter and I unleash the ram, slam hard on the rear brake as I lower my center of gravity so the motorcycle almost lays on its side and then springs up again, closing ground like a shark after a wounded swimmer.

Bad luck can be trumped by an experienced killer and the driver must be bleeding with little way to staunch the flow from his gunshot wound and his arm must be useless now. I can spot the second bodyguard swiveling in the back seat, trying to keep tabs on me while over his shoulder Noel's face has blanched and his eyes are open and filled with fear.

I have to force the driver into a mistake.

Traffic ahead causes the Mercedes to make another clipped right turn down a narrow street and I realize the driver can *only* make right turns, it is too difficult for him to mount a left with just his good arm to spin the wheel. Maybe with a little practice, but he's had none, and I don't think he's used to driving the boss's car anyway.

The frigid weather has kept most pedestrians off the sidewalk, but a few are crossing the street ahead and it is time to make my move. I throttle the motorcycle forward and to the left of the Mercedes, aligning myself with the back bumper, so close to the rear windshield that I can practically smell the breath of the second bodyguard. He has a pistol up, a snub-nosed .38, a show weapon, a gun he has probably never fired and he is afraid, afraid to even take a potshot at me, afraid the gun might kick back and hit him in the face.

As I suspected, the driver is unable to steer into me. I can hear Noel shouting in French in the front seat, but the second bodyguard ignores his pleas, won't take aim, is swiveling in his seat trying to keep an eye on me, and I brake quickly and sweep the bike around the backside of the Mercedes so I am now on the right bumper and the intersection is practically on us and the driver thinks I have made a mistake and now he can bump me off my perch.

He jerks the wheel to the right, oversteering as I believed he would and the front of the car smashes into a parked Peugeot van just shy of the intersection and its inertia keeps it going so it flips wildly and starts tumbling like a pair of dice, smashing into a couple of unfortunate pedestrians, killing them instantly, before sliding belly up to a stop.

In the next moment, I am off the motorcycle and walking calmly, purposefully to the passenger door of the car. It only takes me an instant to crouch down and look at the bleeding, helpless visage of Anton Noel.

"*Aide*—" he mutters a moment before I shoot him in the face.

Men and women race into the street from nearby buildings, bewildered by the sudden eruption of the accident, and somewhere in the distance, the bleating two-note shriek of a French police siren fills the air.

CHAPTER THREE

I STAND AT A PAY PHONE OUTSIDE THE TRAIN STATION IN NAPLES, WAITING FOR IT TO RING. I am angry. The emotion has been brewing inside me for three days, unabated.

I failed. I was sloppy, I was unprepared, and two pedestrians died in Paris because they chose to brave the cold and cross an avenue at the most unfortunate of times. They are dead and here I stand, alive and empty.

Le Monde reported their names as Jerome Coulfret, a forty-five-year-old jeweler, and Jason Baseden, a twenty-eight-year-old fitness instructor. They did not know each other. Further information about them is scant. They are merely a footnote to the professional execution of Anton Noel, the pharmaceutical CIO shot down as he left work in the middle of the afternoon in Paris.

Though I am waiting for it, the phone's ring manages to startle me.

"You are safe?"

Ryan's voice is unemotional, impassive.

"Yes."

"The city is on edge. Investigations are under way."

"I understand."

He pauses, and I wait. There is more he wants to say.

"I have been doing what I do for a quarter of a century. I have no regrets. So tell me why I'm having misgivings about our relationship now."

"I fucked up. What do you want me to say?"

"I want you to say you are committed to your work."

I press the receiver against my forehead and close my eyes. I'd like to tell him I don't need a goddamn lecture—that I'm more angry with myself than he could ever be—but maybe I *do* need to hear it from him. Maybe I do need a good tongue-lashing, a slap in the face. Something, anything to push me back to the surface where I can breathe fresh air again.

"I underestimated the time necessary to complete this job. It won't happen again."

"I'm not assuaged."

"Well, there's nothing I can—"

"You can stop seeing the bookshop owner."

I feel a dull pulse in my ear where the cool plastic of the phone receiver presses against it. I don't know why I'm surprised; a good fence finds out everything about his targets, and similarly knows everything about his assassins. I won't insult him by asking how or why he was tailing me. I know he was right to do so. And I know he was right to tell me to stop seeing Risina.

"I'll take care of it."

He wants to say more, but it is his turn to be circumspect. After a moment, his voice comes through the phone again, softer.

"We should meet. Discuss our strategy for the remainder of the year where we can talk freely. I think it might be time to evaluate a return to work in America."

"Okay."

"A week from today."

"Okay."

There is no need for us to discuss over a telephone where this encounter will take place. We have planned our meetings sequentially. The last one was in Turin. The next one will be here, at the train station in Naples. We always meet at noon.

I'm about to say "goodbye," but the line has gone dead in my hand.

The Piazza Navona is a giant oval surrounding an Egyptian obelisk and a large fountain in the heart of Rome. The emperor Maxentius built the oval in the fourth century as a stadium for chariot races, where losing competitors were often executed before they left the competing ground. I wonder how much blood has been spilled here over the centuries, what forgotten man once stood where I stand, defeated, waiting for a sword to run him through.

Risina is eating lunch alone.

The day is unseasonably warm, and the cafes and shops are crowded. She is waiting for me to join her, but I can't seem to get my feet to move.

This life asks so goddamn much of me and in return, I get what? Solitude. Anonymity. A name hung on me without meaning. Money in an account I rarely touch. Fleeting human connections severed violently, dispassionately. I have become faceless, a living ghost, a walking embodiment of a vengeful god, meting out punishment with remorseless certitude. I have to trick myself into thinking the punishment is deserved, but that's just a minor inconvenience, right?

And the secret—the truth I keep tucked away like a stolen painting—is I *like* it. I like the power, I like the excitement, I like the hunt. My first fence, Vespucci, once said we held a power reserved for God, that we know our target's future long before he or she does. This power wore him down like those heavy stones on the old man's chest, but it is the opposite for me: a lift, a tonic.

The question is: at what cost? At what point does the necessity for some kind of lasting human connection tip the scales away from the thrill, the allure, the power of the hunt? At what point does it tip to an empty nothingness? I'm not sure I know the answer.

An elderly man stands near me, his hand on the back of a bench, watching people as they pass. He wears a simple smile, and his clothes, though old, are pressed and clean. He is humming a tune to himself, something old and classical, a short, happy melody I vaguely recognize. A young woman in her twenties approaches, kisses him warmly on both cheeks, and I only catch a concerned question from her in Italian . . .

"You are warm, Grandfather?"

. . . before they shuffle away. I swallow hard, can feel my hand balling into a fist, can feel the weight in the scales tipping off its median. I sneak one last look at Risina, and, before I make a decision I might regret, I leave the Piazza Navona alone.

In Naples, a week later, I am thumbing through my first-edition copy of *The Compleat Angler*, biding my time while I wait for Ryan to step off the train from Rome.

I have had time to think, to get my mind right, and there is only one solution. There has always been only one solution. I have decided I will tell her. I have to tell her.

I won't need to hear the reproof from Ryan, the judgmental tone in his voice. I know what I have to do. I know the only way the scales can tip.

I will never have grandchildren to comfort me when I'm old, to ask me if I'm warm enough as I stand contentedly in the middle of a crowded square humming a tune. I can't have things that can be taken from me, that can be used as leverage against me. I chose this life, and the cost is mine to bear. I will have to jettison Risina before the sinking ship drowns us both.

I am standing with my back to a corner made by a newspaper stand adjoining the rail-station wall. The terminal is always bustling as passengers try to dodge the thieves, liars, and beggars aiming to separate them from their money. It is easy to fade into the backdrop here.

The train from Rome arrives and I spot Ryan climbing down from one of the middle cars. He is dressed conservatively, as always, but there is something odd about his gait as he heads my way. He's favoring his left leg, limping a bit, and, as he strides closer, I can see one side of his face is swollen and purple.

I head toward him, but he is deliberately looking past me, over my shoulder, at some imaginary person thirty feet behind me, avoiding eye contact completely, and everything about this encounter is wrong.

"Turner!" he says loudly as he approaches, like he's calling out to the phantom behind me. "Jeff!"

Turner. Turner. What's in a name? A pre-planned warning. A signal decided upon when we first went into business together. Ryan has been set up, compromised, and he's letting me know to ignore him, to keep walking, to get the hell out of there as quickly as I can.

I lock eyes on a woman stepping off the train and wave to her like *she's* the one I've been hurrying to see and as I move past Ryan, I hear the unmistakable sound of a bullet whizzing past my ear before it slams squarely into Ryan's back. From the angle of the shot, I know the shooter is ahead of me and as Ryan crumples to the dirty cement, as the crowd on the landing starts to scatter in all directions like shrapnel, I catch just a glimpse of a dark-suited, bearded man holding a pistol two platforms over.

His eyes find mine and it's enough. It was a smart play to take out Ryan as soon as the fence opened his mouth. By shooting him, this professional killer flushes the true target. He drops Ryan and watches the crowd's reaction, focusing in on anyone who looks up at the bullet's flight path instead of scrambling away in a panic. He looks for a professional, a man who doesn't jump at the sound of a gun firing in a crowd. It's what I would have done.

Goddammit, the jig is up; he knows I'm the quarry, the one Ryan was coming to meet. Without thinking, I draw my Glock and unload back at the bearded man, off-balance, knowing instinctively my shots will miss the mark yet give me enough time to duck for cover.

A train is backing away from the station on the tenth platform, and I bolt for it, trying to make myself as small as possible, careful not to run in a straight line. I know enough about putting bullets into people to hopefully avoid the shooter putting one into me.

Anton Noel. The sloppiness of the kill came home to roost. Of course he had friends in high places, friends who wouldn't be encumbered by police procedure or official leads, friends who would hire dark men like me to hunt down and execute the executioner. The man's company counted life and death as numbers on an accountant's ledger, so why should I be surprised someone close to Noel hired a professional to exact revenge? This hired gun got to Ryan and worked him over and Ryan led the bagman to me, but not before he called out for "Jeff Turner," giving me one last professional, undeserved nod, before he died with a bullet in his spine.

I hear a gunshot ricochet off the pavement somewhere near

my right foot but I don't break stride, just zero in on the door to the debarking train. A quick glance over my shoulder reveals the bearded man sprinting my way, out in front of a host of light-blue uniformed Italian Railway Police officers.

"Interpol! Interpol!" he is shouting, but he is no more a part of the international criminal police organization than I am. Interpol agents aren't the swashbuckling lawmen seen in countless films or read about in mystery novels. They don't carry guns, can't make arrests, and rarely leave their offices. His shouting is creating the intended effect amongst the Railway officers, however: confusion.

A few more steps and I bang on the last train door, the pressure causing it to swish open. I leap through it, and immediately crouch next to the luggage rack, pointing my gun up at the doorway, waiting, hoping the bearded man will make a mistake, try to chase me inside, but all I spy through the sliver of the doorway is the last bit of the tenth platform moving away as the train rolls out of the station.

When Risina opens the bookshop, I am already inside.

"My God—"

"I'm sorry. I didn't mean to startle you."

"How did you—?"

"The door was open."

"It was?"

I nod. "I was going to stand outside and wait for you, but when I saw the door, I thought you were already here. I just walked in and you came up behind me."

She looks puzzled, worried. "The alarm—"

"I don't know what to tell you."

She hurries over to the cases of old texts, but no glass has been broken, no volumes appear to be missing.

"I remember—" She stops to curse in Italian. "I thought I locked up like usual."

She shakes her head, her hand flitting to her temples, brushing her long black hair away from her forehead. She looks at me in the middle of the room, like she has just remembered something. "You stood me up. We had a date for lunch."

"I had some unexpected business." I am watching her eyes. "I meant to call, but things happened quickly."

She nods stiffly, and I'm not sure she believes me, as though she's heard that excuse before. That underlying sadness is fluttering just below the surface of her skin again. It doesn't matter; I have cards left to play and despite my own misgivings, I plan on playing them. I don't fully understand why, but I *have* to play them.

"I need to ask you something."

"Yes?"

She moves over to the ornate desk in the back of the room, checking the drawers to see if any have been forced.

"I have to go away for a while. I have to do some things that are important to me, which may require me to leave Italy for some time."

I watch as her shoulders sag a bit, as her head lowers. "I see."

"No, I—" I stop, choosing my words carefully.

She looks up from the desk to meet my eyes, sensing that the words I choose will carry weight.

"It's that . . . my question is this . . ." I can feel my throat tighten. "Will you wait for me?"

CHAPTER FOUR

HOW MUCH IS A NAME WORTH?

In the killing business, names have value. The names of targets can command staggering sums, depending on the difficulty of the assassination. The name of a U.S. cabinet member might be worth more than say, a Wall Street trader or a low-level crime boss. The name of a CEO guarded by a host of expensive and professional bodyguards might be more valuable than a police officer who is about to testify and is too smug or pig-headed to bother with protection. But these aren't the only names in the business of death that hold worth.

Fences, middlemen, go-betweens are hired to keep us from knowing whom we're working for and to keep clients from knowing whom they're hiring. They are windowless walls erected to protect us from ourselves, to keep ends from becoming loose. But there was a breakdown of the wall protecting me; someone used William Ryan's head as a battering ram and knocked right through it. I don't know who that someone is yet, but I plan to find out.

I know a name too.

Doriot is the fence who hired me to kill Anton Noel, the same fence who hired me four times in the past. He's on the acquiring side, meaning he works with clients directly and then selects assassins to fill his jobs.

Before the first assignment, acquiring fences often meet with gunmen so they can kick the tires on the showroom car. They want to get a look and feel for the killer they will be contracting; they want to be able to assure their client they are on top of things, all will go smoothly, they have a relationship with the killer and they trust the job will be cleanly and professionally executed. Clients tend to get jumpy as the contract inches closer to fulfillment; an experienced acquiring fence placates the nervous party by extolling the achievements of the assassin hired to do the job. It always helps to say he knows the gunman personally, even better if he's used the same assassin in the past.

Whether or not Doriot sold out Ryan is immaterial, though he seems the most likely candidate. He's the only direct connection between Noel and me. I don't care about revenge; I'm going to dispassionately put a bullet in whoever hired someone to kill me. It is the only way to take down the contract on my life, to pull the scent away from the hound's nose.

I have two guesses as to the identity of the man who put a price on my head. Either he's someone close to Anton Noel, as I speculated before, or he's the same man who hired me to kill Noel and after the sloppiness of the job, he wants all ties to the assassination severed. Since I'm not sure yet how to tackle the first hypothesis, I'll start with the second.

Brussels is a cold city in the middle of Europe. It is a mixture of old and new, of modern skyscrapers and shopping pavilions and art-deco houses standing shoulder to shoulder with Gothic cathedrals and pristine fifteenth-century town halls. Currently the seat of the European Union's Council and Commission, the city and its people are aloof, taciturn. The entire place feels like a museum that allows you to enter, but asks you to speak softly and not touch anything. It is somewhat telling that Brussels's most popular attraction is a statue of a little boy pissing into a basin.

Doriot lives here. I met him once, in a secure building near the river, about two years ago, before my first assignment for him. Like I said, acquiring fences like to kick the tires, and Doriot wanted to kick mine.

I remember it was cold that day, and I entered the address from a secluded street near the Zenne river. The front door opened and locked behind me, leaving me in a ten-foot-by-ten-foot "holding" room. An intercom in the wall barked at me. The killing business flourishes all over the world, but, conveniently, its agreed-upon universal language is English.

"May I help you?" A baritone voice with a slightly German accent that sounded like it was coming from the bottom of a well filled the room.

"I'm Columbus. I have an appointment with Doriot."

"Step back from the door, empty your chambers, and place your clips on the floor in front of you. Then clasp your fingers behind your head."

Most acquiring fences surround themselves with a small army of protection, at least the prominent ones do if they want to stay prominent. I was used to this. I didn't get defensive, I didn't protest, I just did as commanded without revealing an ounce of emotion on my face.

After a moment, a giant of a man entered through the opaque door in front of me, holding a leather bag. Quietly, he collected the three clips I had placed on the floor, along with the two bullets I had ejected from the chambers of my Glocks. Finished, he turned and faced me.

"Hello, Columbus."

"Hello." I kept my fingers interlocked behind my head.

"I will have to frisk you now. Yes?"

I nodded and he ran his hands over my body, patting me down. I kicked off my shoes and he checked my ankles, then the seams of my pants. His hands were massive, the size of melons. He gave me a thorough examination, then, satisfied, stepped back.

"My name is Brueggemann. I work for Monsieur Doriot. You have heard of me?"

I shook my head and he watched my eyes, checking to see if I was withholding anything. Then he made a "tsk" sound, sucking air between his teeth. "I used to do what you do. Yes? For many years. Over twenty. Yet I am still here."

"Not many can say that." I thought this was what he wanted to hear. Challenging strangers at this stage of the game is foolish, a good way to get yourself in a bad way.

He nodded. "No, not many. Now I work safety for the boss. And the boss is always safe, you understand?"

I shrugged, keeping my expression a well-practiced neutral. "I'm just here to pick up my assignment. I have no interest in tearing down fences."

He smiled, revealing a gap in his front teeth I could've driven a rig through. His eyes didn't smile, though; they stayed chained to mine. "You may see Monsieur Doriot now. Make sure you do not approach him. Yes?"

I lowered my arms and straightened out my jacket. "Not a problem."

I was ushered in to see the boss, a small man with awkward frameless glasses perched on his nose. He was sitting behind an oversized desk. Brueggemann never left my side. I answered the usual questions impassively, while Doriot studied me the way a rancher examines a prize bull. He had heard about the jobs I'd pulled in the States, had heard about my reputation, and a few pointed answers to his questions let him know I had done the work Ryan claimed. I had the feeling he wanted to ask more, to try to open me up, but he knew the futility in that, and so gave me my assignment and had Brueggemann show me to the door.

The next day, I cased the building, invisible in the shadows of a nearby alley. Names hold value and Brueggemann had given me his, ostensibly to advertise his reputation. But if he had once been a contract killer like me, he had lost a step, gone soft in his retirement, the way a moonlighting cop lets his defenses down when he's sitting on a security guard's stool. It was a mistake giving me his name. The cons outweighed the pros; the scales tipped away from his favor. I knew his boss Doriot would be careful to avoid detection or pursuit when he entered or exited the building in Brussels where he did business . . . he was a deliberate and methodical professional. He would vary his routine, have multiple entrance and exit points, take illogical routes to wherever he laid his head. Ours is a business where reputation is prized but anonymity is essential. We have to be able to float into this world, this game, and then shut the door behind us when we leave. A private, personal life can never be fully realized, I have learned this all too well, but we can do things to make the likelihood of clashes between the two worlds, if not impossible, at least improbable. Still, I hoped Brueggemann's lack of foresight in revealing his name would mean he was lax when covering his own tracks.

I didn't have to wait long to find out. He exited the building through the same door I had entered the day before and headed north up the street, toward the city center, walking with his hands in his pockets, not even checking over his shoulder or scanning shop windows for reflections. Being as big as he was, he was as easy to follow as if he'd been painted red. I hung back and stayed with him until he retreated into a three-story apartment building only a quarter of a mile from the office. A minute later, a light came on in a corner window on the top floor. Brueggemann had led me right to his doorstep.

So why did I follow him?

Because names hold value, and you never know when you'll need to collect a trinket from your safe.

Two years later, and I am waiting in his hallway when he lumbers to his door. He has his hands in his pockets and is humming a song I don't recognize.

"Hello, Brueggemann."

He turns his head at the sound, slowly. Being so large, every movement he makes takes an eternity. His eyes find the gun in my hand and then flit back to my face. The only flicker of emotion he gives is a slight pursing of his lips.

"I remember you."

"Good."

"Columbus, yes?"

"Yes."

He pulls his hands out of his pockets and takes a small step toward his apartment. In his left hand, he's holding a set of keys.

He looks ahead, like he's speaking to the door. He is trying to keep his voice even, relaxed. "The boss told me many things about the work you've done. He said you were particularly good with . . ."

And then he swings away from the door and towards my face, lunging with his left, the keys leading the way.

I wanted this to happen, and I don't blame him for trying. If I had come on strong, kept my distance and then ordered him away with my gun in his back, he would have made an attempt to challenge me at some point. It's better to get it done early, break the man's spirit, so the remainder of our time together can be spent usefully.

One of the things I learned at the Waxham detention center was to fight dirty against older and bigger opponents. Many believe the best way to take down a big man is to drive your heel into his kneecap, buckling it, chopping his legs out from under him so he'll fall like a redwood. This always sounds good in theory, but the reality is it takes a precise, well-balanced kick, and if you miss above or below, then you're either striking thick thigh muscle or the rock-hard bones of the shin. It's not easy to do in a juvey yard, much less in the tight confines of a Brussels apartment corridor.

No, the preferable strike points are one of two places. The groin is excellent, on both men and women, and with enough impact, a single strike can sap the fight out of even the roughest of giants. But Brueggemann is swinging wildly, and the hallway isn't all that well lit and I don't want to miss his crotch, so I go for the second option.

The little light available in the hall reflects off the fleshy white skin of his neck and I quickly duck his arm and pop him with everything I have square in the throat.

The results are immediate, the keys go flying and he collapses to both knees, clutching his gullet while he sucks desperately for air. His face turns crimson, his eyes roll back and fill with tears, his breath sounds like a cat mewing.

I just wait.

Finally, he's able to get some air back into his lungs and he looks over at me, defeat sweeping across his face like a bitter wind. He shrugs, still on his knees.

"What . . . do you want?"

"I want you to take me to Doriot. I want you to lead me to your boss where I can get to him and I don't want him to know I'm coming. Do you understand?"

"Yes." And inexplicably, a small grin creases his face, revealing that big gap between his front teeth.

We stand in Lantin, about 60 miles west of Brussels, outside of the jailhouse. It is a blocky building, one of those holdovers from the sixties that were made with little imagination.

Brueggemann has his arms folded across his chest.

"When?"

"Three weeks ago. The police stormed a restaurant he was dining in. . . ."

"Where were you?"

"He said he needed to be alone."

"Convenient."

"Yes."

I look over at the bodyguard, who keeps a smug expression on his face. "You think he wanted to be caught?"

"He didn't pay me enough to think."

I shake my head. It is frigid outside, but my face feels warm, flush with blood.

"You speak to him since?"

"Not a word."

"Goddammit." I look at the prison, shaking my head.

Brueggemann speaks up. "You will let me go now, yes?"

I nod, and he doesn't wait for more. He spins and marches back in the direction of the town without a backward glance.

Carrots or sticks.

I stand against a wall in the prison yard in Lantin, waiting for Doriot to come out. I am dressed in the yellow jumpers assigned to all Belgian prisoners, my hands in my pockets, my toes numb from the cold. Mostly, the night is as black as coal, but occasionally the moon makes a brief appearance before ducking back to safety.

Often in doing what I do, there is information I need, or travel arrangements I must have, or access to a building I must be granted. I can't do it alone; I rely upon strangers to get me the things I require. And so I have to decide in each instance which avenue is the best to get me where I want to go: the carrot, or the stick? A bribe, or a threat?

I didn't want to take too long to get to Doriot. That bearded man is still hunting me, and the way he worked over Ryan suggests he got ample information before he shot him in the back. I own a home in Positano along the Amalfi coast of Italy, and I imagine the man who flushed me in Naples surely went there next.

An official visitation with Doriot would've been insufficient. Three feet of bulletproof glass separating us would render any threat moot. I had to get inside where I could work him close.

It didn't take me long to find out which bar the Lantin guards frequented. A place known simply as "The Pub" featured television screens showing rugby, soccer, and cricket, with taps that served

Stella, Jupiler, Hoegaarden and Leffe. I stood at the bar and mumbled to a waitress in English and watched the shifts change and the prison guards mope in for three straight days. I didn't know Dutch and only minimal French, but I've found reading faces is as important as speaking. I wanted a sap, a guy with the most hang-down expression stamped on his mug like an advertisement for desperation. And I wanted a guy with a family.

On the third day, I clocked the same man coming off the night shift, a sad-sack, overweight guy with a moony face expressing a permanent look of bewilderment. On my way out, I asked him for a lighter in English without making any hand gestures and he produced one from his two-pocket shirt. He spoke English, or at least understood it, and that would help.

He rode a Vespa and I followed him from a casual distance until he reached a tiny apartment resembling a college dormitory. His wife barked at him from a window before he even cut the engine of his bike. She was holding an infant. He would do.

I stood in his living room when he came out of his bathroom, wiping his hands on his pants. His eyes had trouble conveying to his brain what he was seeing, a stranger in his living room, holding a pistol in one hand and a stack of cash in the other. His wife was in the bedroom, breast-feeding the baby.

"I need a favor from you."

His eyes wouldn't leave my hands, as though his neurons had stopped firing, his mind had shut down. Finally, he searched my face for some sort of sign he wasn't hallucinating.

"I'm going to need you to get me inside the jail and bring a prisoner to me in the north yard, alone."

He blinked, but nothing came out of his mouth.

"If you do this for me, you'll have the ten thousand euros in my right hand and you'll never see me again. If you fail, or you fuck me in any way, then your wife and your baby are going to get what's in my left. Nod your head if you understand."

Carrots or sticks. Sometimes, if you want to be sure, you choose both.

I can hear Doriot coming before he rounds the corner. He is spitting curses in French, propelled against his will by the moon-faced guard I threatened. He had probably just racked out for the night in his cot and was surprised to be awoken, singled out, and shuffled outside to the yard.

He turns the corner and his eyes peel open, all signs of sleep vanishing. His adam's apple bobs as he swallows dryly. He reels back against the guard, but the man holds him there, firm.

"Hello, Doriot."

Doriot tries to swivel his head to meet the guard's eyes. "He's a killer! He's here to kill me." But the guard just shuffles away.

"That's debatable. Why'd you sell Ryan down the river?"

It doesn't matter what his response is, I'm watching his eyes. His French accent is thick; it seems to pull his whole face down when he speaks, but his eyes don't waver or blink. "I didn't . . . you have no right accusing me of this thing, Columbus."

"Your client wants me dead."

His eyes slide back and forth, like he's puzzled, searching for an answer. "What is this you're telling me?"

"The man who hired me to put a bullet in Anton Noel."

"Yes?"

"He's upset."

"Why should he be upset? You fulfilled the contract."

"It was sloppy."

There is a glint of hope in Doriot's eyes now, like he can sense we aren't on the same page and his life might be spared because of it. "Sloppy? What is this *sloppy*? My client would have cared nothing if you'd blown up a rail platform with five hundred people on it just to kill that bastard Noel."

I chew on this, turning it over in my mind so I can see it from all angles. The little man in front of me isn't faking his response. I believe him. Or at least I believe he isn't involved. But that's a far cry from his client not being involved. His client might have been equally upset with Doriot and not used his services for this particular bit of cleaning up.

"Why'd you let yourself get thrown in here?"

"Reasons that have nothing to do with you."

"You see how easily I got to you?"

He lowers his eyes. "Yes. That does concern me. Yes."

"What is your client's name?"

"You know that I cannot—"

"If he's happy as you say he is, then he'll never know I was barking up his tree. If he's not happy and hasn't included you, then it'd be in your best interest for me to get to him. Before he gets to you."

I can see the wheels turning behind his eyes as he maps the various moves in his head like a chess player trying to envision the board ten plays ahead. Finally, he nods.

"His name is Thomas Saxon. He's an American. I have worked for him more than once. He is a hard man."

"I know all about hard men. What city?"

"Atlanta."

"All right then." I nod at the guard, who comes back over, looking relieved. He starts to whirl Doriot back the way he came.

"Wait," the little man says, and the guard stops for a moment. Doriot looks over his shoulder at me. "What happened to Ryan?"

"Shot in the spine in the Naples train station."

He gnaws on his lip for a second, then nods at the guard. As their footsteps recede and the prison yard falls silent, I turn my eyes up to the nameless moon right before it disappears behind a cloud.

CHAPTER FIVE

HE'S TOYING WITH ME.

I've seen the bearded man twice since leaving Belgium. First, I thought I'd lucked into spotting him at the Gatwick airport. I was walking through the terminal, heading to catch a cab to Heathrow, airport-hopping so I could fly directly to Atlanta. I took a turn at the last moment, realizing the taxi stand was to the left, and I caught his reflection behind me in the glass window of a coffee klatch.

I have trained myself not to flinch. Ever. Not to hesitate, not to give a moment's pause. He had scented my trail faster than I thought possible, but now he'd made a mistake. I lined up in the taxi queue, checked my wrist like I was looking at my watch, and then ducked into the baggage claim so I could stand behind the carousel and watch the only two entranceways into the room. He never came through the doors.

I waited patiently, then quickly bought a tan coat from an Austin Reed store and pitched my gray one in a trashcan. It wasn't much, but maybe it would steal me a moment, and sometimes a moment is all I need.

I didn't see him again that day. I switched flights and holed up at the Savoy on the Strand, spending two days in the lobby reading, watching the door. He never showed and I started to doubt whether I had actually seen him in Gatwick. It had only been a moment, a split second, just his face some forty feet behind me, and how could I be sure, really sure it was him?

Because my life had always relied on these moments of perspicacity. If I started to doubt them now, I might as well quit, really quit. I might as well head back to Rome, scoop up Risina Lorenzana and try to disappear where no one would ever find us. But I couldn't do that, not now. Someone with a gun was looking for me and in my experience, hiding would only delay the inevitable. Instead of trying to outrun him, never knowing when he'd catch me, I needed to turn my boat and steer into him with everything I had. Let the crash determine which of us swims away free.

I saw him the second time in Atlanta at the Lenox mall. I pitched my tent at the Sheraton in Buckhead and headed to the shops to give my wardrobe an overhaul. It was teeth-chattering cold in Georgia, and the tickling at the back of my neck told me to ditch everything I'd worn in Europe and start over, buy casual clothes and blend into the background, especially if I was going to be spending time in the South.

I was riding up an escalator, exposed, vulnerable, when I saw him on the first-floor landing, looking directly at me. Smiling. If he wanted to pop me there, he could have. Hell, he *should* have. Which begged the question, how many times had he gotten this close since Naples and not finished the kill? I instinctually ducked down to tie my shoe, riding out the rest of the escalation below the shooter's sight line. I kept low, acting like I was tugging my socks up and practically crawled into Macy's like a crab darting across the sand. I didn't want to get cornered in a store with only one entrance and exit. I needed options, quickly.

The department store had its own escalators in the center of the clothing area, but standing exposed and upright on a moving staircase is a dangerous game, as I had just been reminded. Instead, I ducked to the back of the store and zeroed in on a pair of elevators, usually reserved for women with strollers. Doors were just closing as I hustled aboard and pressed the button for the bottom floor of underground parking.

I waited there for over an hour, in an obscure corner with no traffic, freezing my ass off. I didn't see him again.

In my hand, I'm holding a Nokia pre-paid cell phone I picked up at a mini-mart near the Holiday Inn in Decatur where I'm now staying. I employed every anti-surveillance technique I know in driving away from Buckhead, veering on and off the highway, racing red lights, making unexpected turns, and I'm pretty sure I haven't been followed, but I'm not positive, goddammit, and this fucker has me doubting myself in ways I have not doubted in a long time.

And yet, if he wanted to kill me, if that was his end game, then he made a colossal mistake in not doing so when he had the chance. If he's so fucking smug that he's choosing to play games, choosing to reveal himself so that I know *he* knows where I am, then I'm going to pluck whatever weapon he comes at me with right out of his hands and ram it down his fucking throat. Toying with your target is a novice's play, a cocksure move intended to intimidate your mark into making a mistake. But there are flaws to this play, and chief amongst them is that he has given away information about himself.

My pursuer carries a knife in his left sleeve, I'm sure of it. In the two instances where I spotted him, I took in the folds of his jacket, and both times, the left sleeve bunched up near the wrist opening, then smoothed out toward the elbow. It wasn't much, and I'd only had a second to look, but it was there.

Maybe he has been paid not just to kill me, but to stick me up close, to disfigure me, a vendetta killing. I've heard of bagmen taking this kind of work, not just ending a mark's life, but disgracing him in death, pissing on his grave. Come to think of it, it would require the killer to work in close, and maybe that's why he'd been aiming low in the train station in Naples, when the bullet skipped off the pavement by my feet. Maybe he had been aiming for my knees, hoping to wing me so he could carve me up like beef at the slaughterhouse. Or maybe I don't know what the fuck I'm talking about.

I dial a number from memory, look at the digital clock next to my bed, and wait for her to answer.

"*Ciao?*"

"Risina. It's Jack Walker."

Her voice warms immediately. I can feel the smile through the phone line.

"*Buongiorno,* Jack. I was just opening the store."

"I thought you might be. Do you have a moment?"

"Yes. Yes. How are you?"

"I'm . . . fine."

"You don't sound fine."

"I don't? I'm tired, I guess."

"Where are you?"

"The States. East Coast."

"It is late there."

"Yes."

"Well, I'm very pleased you called. I was thinking about you."

"I'm glad you were. I think about you too much."

She laughs. It is a sound low in her throat, as soothing as a touch. "You can never think about me too much, Jack."

I wait for a moment, and there is an odd comfort in the silence, like the distance between us has been erased. I don't know why I feel the compulsion to say what I'm about to say, but the words come out of me before I can decide against them.

"I was just remembering a story I read once. Something from when I was a kid."

"Yes?"

"Maybe you can figure out for me who wrote it."

"I can try. It is a children's story?"

"Well, I read it when I was a kid, but I'm not sure where or how

I came across it. I'm not sure how old I was when I read it. A lot of those years are blurry for me."

"It's a famous story?"

"I'm not sure. I don't think so. I haven't come across it in a long time. But some things in my life made me think of this story, and I thought maybe I'd tell it to you and see if you'd heard of it. I'm not even sure if it's very good or particularly profound."

"Well, now I'm definitely intrigued. Let's hear it." I hear the sound of her leaning back in the desk chair, and I picture her with her knees pulled to her chest and one arm around them, holding them tight, those venerable leather-bound books surrounding her like a theater audience. "I haven't unlocked the shop door yet and Alda is not coming in until after lunch. My ear is yours."

"Okay. Well, here goes. I don't remember the name of the story. And the main character doesn't have a name. In fact, that's the point of the story . . . I think . . . anyway. . . ."

"I'm listening. . . ."

"Well, this guy, just a normal guy, he kisses his wife good-bye, leaves his house, dressed like he's going out for a jog, but he's not, he's actually got his kid in his arms, a little boy, a two-and-a-half-year-old toddler who looks just like him.

"And every day they do this . . . he and his kid take a walk together, all over the city. Or rather, he walks, pulling a silver wagon with his kid buckled safely inside. And they walk everywhere, I mean everywhere, looking at the fire trucks and the police cars and the ambulances and the construction trucks; and all the time, the dad's pointing out this thing and that thing and the kid's taking it all in like a sponge.

"The dad'll pull him for hours, for miles, end up in neighborhoods nowhere near his own, and everyone that passes them on the sidewalk or in the street looks at the two of them longingly and thinks that this father and this son who resemble each other are just a little part of the world that is right. That all the death and mayhem and war and assassinations and everything else wrong in this world is pulling them into the blackest of abysses, but this thing, these two walking by, father and son, these two are what's honest and true and hopeful. And maybe they're the *only* two, you know? Maybe everybody else has a little blackness in his life, but it all fades away to white, because when people spot this guy and his son walking down the street, they just can't help but smile."

I can hear her breathing, but she doesn't cough or sigh or interrupt. I can't remember the last time I've talked this much, but the words continue to tumble out of my mouth like an avalanche.

"And they're on this block a good mile from their house and the dad is in the middle of telling his son about this big cedar tree on the end of the street he likes to visit, that the tree probably looks to the boy like it's taller than a skyscraper, and right there, right in the middle of his sentence, the man's left arm seizes up on him, his breath catches in his throat, and he falls down dead. Heart attack, no warning, right there on the sidewalk. He topples over like someone shot him and lies face down on the concrete.

"The kid doesn't know what's going on, he's only two and a half. Is the father playing some sort of game with him? That's all this kid knows. So he calls out to his dad, 'Da-ad. Da-ad.' You know, like it's a song, like it's a game. But his father doesn't, his father *can't* get up.

"'Something is wrong' registers in the kid's brain . . . even caught in the middle between two and three, this message comes through loud and clear, but he can't get out of the silver wagon, he's stuck there, buckled in tight. He starts blinking tears, crying in that way toddlers cry, his lips curved in an 'o,' his wail silent then strong then silent again as he can't catch his breath to pound it out.

"And then a man comes up, this homeless guy, this guy who reeks of alcohol and cigarettes and the kid thinks at first maybe this man will help him, help his dad, who is still lying face down on the sidewalk, but the raggedy man descends like a vulture, his eyes darting, he barks at the kid to 'shut the hell up' as he's rifling through the father's pockets and there's not a damn thing the kid can do about it.

"The guy takes what he can and hurries away, leaving the kid, the boy who isn't much more than a baby sitting there in the silver wagon, stuck there, a mile from home, where he can't see anything but his father lying there dead on the sidewalk and still no one has noticed. No one has come for him. The mother is oblivious in a house a mile away and the father and son are gone for hours sometimes and she's still forty-five minutes away from even thinking something's wrong.

"The kid starts to cry again, because he's scared now even if he doesn't know why, but he's scared in that part of him where deep, deep down through centuries and centuries of ingrained behavior we know we're in danger even before we are.

"And right then, just as he's getting worked up to really wail, a woman comes rushing out of her house. She'd just been looking out the window and saw that kid and that wagon stuck on the sidewalk and the man fallen over and he hasn't gotten up and she rushes over to check on the man, and she feels for a pulse, but she knows he's dead, and so quickly she has that seatbelt unbuckled and has the kid up and in her arms and she's saying 'it's okay, it's okay. What's your name, child? What's your name? Can you tell me your name?'

"And the kid knows his name, he does, it's on the tip of his tongue, his parents have called him it a thousand times and he's said it himself a few times too, but it won't come out, he can't make it come out and so he just shakes in her arms, sobbing."

I sit there for a moment, listening for her on the other end of the phone.

"That's it. That's what I remember."

Her breathing has stopped, like she's afraid to exhale. After a long moment, she breaks the silence. "I wish I could tell you I knew this story. But I don't."

"Yeah. I haven't been able to track it down."

"Well I like it. I like it very much. I need to think about it some more. Consult some other sources."

"If it's not too much trouble."

"No trouble at all."

"Well, thank you. I really appreciate that, Risina."

"Are you certain you're okay?"

"Yes, I'm certain."

"I'm very glad you called me, Jack. I'm still thinking of this story. I can see why it stuck with you."

"Yes."

We talk for another ten minutes about nothing before we say our goodbyes. I head into the bathroom, wrap the phone inside a towel, and then smash it with the heel of my shoe until it shatters into pieces. Slowly, methodically, I flush each piece down the toilet.

Thomas Saxon isn't quite a billionaire, but he doesn't mind when people make that mistake. He's a vulture investor, a corporate raider, a man who never found a shortcut he wouldn't take. He was a frequent attendee of the Predator's Ball in Los Angeles in the eighties, when a few men created enormous wealth by building an entire financial market around junk bonds. Information was key—whether it could be gained legally or illegally didn't matter. The SEC caught up with a few, others escaped scot-free, entire companies were carved up, chewed up, and spit out, but everyone involved made the kind of money that has strings of zeroes at the end of the number. The suckers were the ones who worked within the system, and the suckers never came out on top. Tommy Gun, as his friends called him, was nobody's sucker.

He is living in an enormous house in East Atlanta, out past the airport. It was originally built for Evander Holyfield's mother, but after she died, the champ didn't want to set foot in it again. Saxon paid cash and moved in within a week of the funeral.

Like a lot of financial guys, Saxon thinks he is invincible, immune to the dangers that felled some of his friends and rivals. He narrowly dodged charges from the SEC in 1987 while he watched his associates drop like flies. He thought he was untouchable, special, lucky. This feeling of grandeur ultimately manifested in the hiring of dark men like me. How many men Tommy Gun has sentenced to death, I have no idea. Does he do it because of petty rivalries? Out of hubris? Or is it all just about money? I don't have a fence to put files together for me, so the information I have is only what I can cobble together over the Internet or through an assortment of shadow guys I've come into contact with over the years. I am beginning to suspect Anton Noel meant nothing more to Saxon than numbers across a ticker, that his death was engineered to affect the price of Ventus-Safori's stock. Yet, I feel a nagging at the back of my brain, like something doesn't want to add up so easily, like the square peg is just a little too unwieldy to fit inside the round hole.

Often, an assassin will get to a mark through his vices. A guy might have a mistress, or visit a regular whore, and since he has to be sneaky about meeting the woman, he compromises himself, makes himself as easy to pick off as a duck at a broken-down shooting gallery. He might enjoy a specific type of cigar, or a certain bottle of wine, or participate in an illicit card game, and a contract killer can get to him by posing as a delivery guy or a rival gambler. Everyone has vulnerabilities; it is an assassin's job to exploit them.

Saxon doesn't keep a mistress, smoke cigars, or play poker. He doesn't visit whores or collect French wines or smoke a little weed on the side. No, what Saxon likes to do is fish.

Every weekend, he drives an hour north of Atlanta, into the mountains, alone, and fly-fishes the Soque River. Fishing is a solitary endeavor, a chance for him to commune with nature. Maybe he does it because it brings back memories of him and his old man casting their lines. Maybe he does it to get out of the rat race and clear his mind. Or maybe he thinks stepping into the water will somehow wash his sins down the river.

I tail him for three straight weekends before determining the Soque River as the place our lives will intersect.

I am standing in the men's room of a tiny store named Ramsey's Bait and Tackle off of Highway 197 in the town of Jackson Bridge. A biting wind has kept most anglers near a warm fire this weekend, but not Saxon. Every Saturday, he makes the trek north, no matter the icy temperature or thick frost on the ground.

Saxon hasn't yet come to the store, but he'll be here soon. I take a quick look in the mirror and set my jaw, steeling myself, getting ready. The bell over the door in the front of the shop jingles.

I turn on the water of the sink and position myself behind the bathroom door so I'll be hidden when he enters. I take one last breath as the handle starts to bend downward. If I were waiting for Saxon, this would be over in moments. But I'm not waiting for Saxon.

It is common to use a shiny lure to catch trout, letting the sun filter down through the murky water until the bait catches the fish's eye and suckers him toward the hook.

For the last two weeks, I made a show of stalking Saxon. I watched him out in the open, paced the perimeter of his office, followed him out to his favorite fishing spot in a red SUV. I was letting the sun reflect off me, hoping to reel in my catch.

The door to the restroom pushes open and the bearded man is

coming through cautiously but not cautiously enough. I grab his head and the back of his pants and drive him head-first into the bathroom mirror, shattering it, cutting a red streak across his forehead. He's a professional—up until two seconds ago a pretty goddamn *smug* professional—and he immediately tries to counter, wailing backward with his left elbow, but I move with the blow and use his own inertia against him, whipping him around for a second meeting with what's left of the mirror.

He's got heart, I'll give him that. He drops like a rock, plunging to the linoleum floor as he tries to whip my feet out from under me but I sidestep his scissoring legs and stomp with everything I have on top of his kneecap until the bones crunch like gravel. He wails in pain, instinctively, and reaches into his sleeve for his knife but it's not there. He looks puzzled for a moment until his eyes settle on my hand.

"You stupid fuck." I am holding his knife in one hand and my pistol in the other.

"Let's work something out, Columbus," he says from the ground, his hands raised, his right leg snapped at an angle like a wishbone. He's got a thick Irish accent that lends a strange softness to his words. His voice doesn't match his face in the least.

"What part of me were you supposed to take back to your client?"

He measures me, trying to determine if he should lie. He also wants to keep me talking; as long as I'm talking, he's alive. I would have tried the same thing.

"Your trigger finger."

"Kill me first and then the finger?"

"Aye, cut it off while you're alive, but yes, that's it."

He lowers one elbow to the ground, leaning back, breathing hard, blinking blood out of his eyes. It is seeping down the contours of his face and collecting in his beard so the whiskers turn a blacker shade, creating an odd aura around his face, like he's getting younger before my eyes. His hand creeps toward his side like an inchworm, but I don't shift my eyes to it.

"You the only one Saxon hired, or are there more?"

"Who's Saxon?" The inchworm keeps inching.

"The guy who's going to call all this off."

"If you say so, brother." Inching. Inching.

"I say so."

And the worm reaches his belt, and in a blur the bearded man has a gun in his hand but my first silenced bullet takes off the top part of his hand, sending the gun skittering across the linoleum until it comes to a rest next to the toilet.

He looks at me with true shock in his eyes just a moment before my second bullet closes them forever.

CHAPTER SIX

THE SPOT ON THE SOQUE RIVER WHERE SAXON LIKES TO FISH IS PRIVATE, PART OF A FISHERMEN'S LODGE THAT HAS BEEN STANDING FOR GENERATIONS. SECURITY IS LAUGHABLE, RELIANT ON A FEW "NO TRESPASSING / PRIVATE PROPERTY" SIGNS AND TWO GUARDS WITH SNOWY HAIR AND BULGING BELLIES, AS THREATENING AS FIELD MICE.

I step out of a small copse and stand directly behind Saxon. He looks like he wandered out of an L.L.Bean catalogue, standing on the bank of the river, wearing navy waders and a plaid hunter's shirt underneath a thick multi-pocketed vest. He is tying a spinner on his line, pulling the knot tight with his teeth as I approach.

"Catch anything?"

He gives me a once-over, like I've just befouled his sanctuary.

"No."

Then he turns his back on me, as if I might disappear. When I don't, he sighs dramatically before looking at me again.

"You staying at the lodge?"

"No."

"Well, this is private property, buddy. And I like fishing alone.".

"I caught something this morning."

"Good for you."

"You might want to take a look at it."

He waits, and I can see the thoughts warring behind his eyes: do I humor this asshole and maybe he'll go away, or do I tell him to get the fuck out of here and possibly incite him? The first choice must win out. Resigned, he offers, "Okay. Show me your catch."

I toss something at his chest and he fumbles his pole as he tries to get his hands on it. When he looks down at his palm, he realizes he is holding a man's finger.

He drops it like it's toxic and stammers, "What is this?"

"The trigger finger of one of your hired killers."

Fear sweeps across his face and his cheeks burn as though they've been slapped.

"Call them off."

"What?"

"The fence you're currently using. Tell him to call off the contract."

"I ... I don't. ..."

"Don't insult me, Tommy. I've already gotten to Doriot in Belgium. I know you're behind this."

I can see terror in his eyes, true fright. This is not at all uncommon in clients who hire killers. More often than not, they are feckless men, men who like to give orders from a safe distance without ever entering the battlefield. They imagine they have courage—ordering the deaths of others through multiple chains of command—but that courage evaporates like boiled water as soon as they come face to face with a man who pulls the trigger. So much for being a hard man. Saxon is as hard as a minnow.

I lower my hands into my pockets conspicuously. His eyes widen as he imagines what I hold there.

"No checking out, no going to the lodge. Just walk out of here slowly, and I'll follow you to my car. You arrange a meeting with the fence on the way. We go together and we end this. Nod if you understand."

"Yes, sir. I understand." He looks like he has something more he wants to add, but he's afraid to open his mouth. I nod to him. "My lawyer is the one who arranges everything with the ... um ... other guys."

"Fine. Your lawyer, then. Let's move."

The drive back is silent. Most men in his situation try to chat me up, to make themselves appear likable, misunderstood, human. But not Tommy Gun. No, he steers the wheel with a scowl on his face, like an unrepentant sinner forced to sit in a Sunday morning service.

He's afraid of me, yes, so he turns that fear to anger. The miles roll beneath the tires and he simmers, a pot of water about to boil over. If he's waiting for me to say something, to break the silence, he's misjudged me. Keeping men like him uncomfortable is a skill, and one I'll admit I enjoy using.

His lawyer's name is Colin Goldman and he lives in Buckhead, not far from the mall where the bearded man watched me on the escalator, smiling when he should have been shooting. Colin is a small man with a big house.

We stand in the grass of the back yard, a good distance from the rear porch. The lawyer is shivering, wearing a robe over a T-shirt and boxer shorts, his feet in slippers. I didn't give him an opportunity to change after he answered the door.

"How many gunmen did you hire?"

Goldman coughs into his fist, nervous. He searches Saxon's face. "I would advise you not to—"

"Tell him."

"He could be a Fed."

"He's not a Fed. Look at his eyes. He's a goddamn killer. Tell him." Saxon's confidence is back, now that he has someone smaller than him to lord over.

Goldman blows out a measured breath. "Ummm . . . just one."

"Well, your one is dead. I shot him in the bathroom of a fishing store in Jackson Bridge."

"Jackson Bridge?" The lawyer looks confused.

"He wanted to get in close, so I let him get in close. Then I shot him in the face."

"I . . . I don't understand."

"I don't give a shit. You hired one and you failed. You should've known better than to send a cut-up man after me. Now, I don't give a fuck if you didn't like the way I worked the Noel job. I finished it, and it's done. You want payback, you poked the wrong animal."

"Wait, what're you talking about?"

It is my turn to feel uncomfortable. An uneasy feeling is starting to settle in my stomach. Square peg, round hole. Men in their positions usually look shamed, crestfallen, like they got caught in the act and are on their way to the guillotine. But these two are genuinely surprised, genuinely bewildered.

"You sent a man after me."

Goldman stammers as he stamps his feet. "We . . . we only have one open job, I swear it. We're taking out an SEC officer. In New York."

Saxon speaks up. "We understand the Noel job was successful. Why would we—?"

In an instant, I have a pair of Glocks up in either hand and am pointing them point-blank at both of their foreheads. A well-positioned gun held in a steady hand makes a hell of a lie detector.

They draw back instinctively. "Ho! I swear it. Whoever you are, we have no beef with you. You have to believe us."

I backhand the lawyer with the barrel of my pistol, so he goes down in a heap, and then I point both barrels at Saxon. The fear in his eyes is pellucid, tangible. He cringes, and there is anger in his voice.

"Goddammit, listen to me. I don't know who you are or what you believe I did, but if you think I put a price on your head, you've never been more wrong. I know my targets, all of them. Y-you got this one wrong." He breathes hard, like he just ran a marathon. "Noel is dead and that case is closed. No reprisals. You got this one wrong."

Here comes that wave again, that bad-luck wave that has dogged me since Paris. Bad luck because this isn't ending in Atlanta, not in the back yard of a little man's big house in Buckhead. And certainly not ending in the bathroom of the Ramsey Bait and Tackle Shop off of Highway 197. Bad luck because where one killer fails, others will surely follow until I find out who has done the hiring. Bad luck because now I know Saxon and the bearded man were telling the truth.

The silver wagon has stopped, the handle has dropped, and I have a name but I don't know it. It has to be in front of me, somewhere. But where, goddammit?

I know the Noel job triggered this. The heat that assignment brought led someone to Ryan, and Ryan led that someone to me. So it had to be a man who knew Ryan fenced for me on that job, and the only link in that chain is Doriot.

Replaying my conversation with the Belgian fence, I remember he was quick to go where I led him, to finger his client, Saxon. In retrospect, it was too easy. Someone had gotten to Doriot first, before me, which is why he got himself tossed in jail. He was just buying time, as much as possible, till this whole thing washed over. He's going to regret having misled me.

The bearded man made a solid play initially, taking out Ryan to get to me. Even though he lost the war, he dealt me a crippling blow. Losing my fence, my middleman, is like missing a limb. I need information, someone to bang an idea off of, someone who can root around in the dirt for a bit and get back to me with a truffle.

The last time I saw a fence named Archibald Grant, he was in the process of hiring me to kill the Speaker of the House of Representatives. But Grant withheld some information at the time of the assignment, namely, that he was asked to hire three assassins instead of just me. My friend and fence Pooley died because of this omission, gunned down in my hotel room in Santa Fe, New Mexico, in the middle of my assignment. I would say Archibald owes me a pretty damn big chit.

Archibald served sixteen months in Lompoc on an aiding-and -abetting collar, but within eight hours of his release, he was back in the game, contacting his old associates, setting up new contracts. Boston must've been too hot for him; he relocated to Chicago, where he has had little difficulty pitching a new tent. It is just as well; I have too many memories floating around Boston.

When he steps out of his bathroom wearing only a towel and shuffles into his kitchen, I am sitting at his breakfast table.

"Fuck me!" Archibald jumps like he's seen a ghost, then covers his heart with his hand, trying to calm himself. He takes a long look at me, recognition in his eyes. "Well, I'll be goddamned. Columbus."

"How you doing, Cotton?"

That takes him by surprise. He hasn't heard his given name, Cotton, in a long time.

"You know that one, huh?"

"I know a lot of things."

"You pop my bodyguards downstairs? The doorman too?" He makes the trigger-pulling gesture with his fingers when he says the word *pop*.

"Nah. They don't even know I'm here."

"Motherfucking Columbus. I heard you lit out of here after the Abe Mann blam-blam. Went to Europe or some shit. I would've put you to work, man, but . . . ." He reaches into his refrigerator and pulls out a jug of milk before moving over to the kitchen table to sit across from me, never finishing the sentence.

"Yeah? I'm splitting time."

He takes a pull straight from the jug, then wipes his mouth with the back of his hand.

"Well, I'm sure you were sore 'bout the way the business was the business. But I was only following orders. And I paid your new boy Ryan triple fee. That may not make it all the way square but it puts some shape on the edges, I would say."

"I need some information."

Archibald smiles. "That's what I do."

"That's why I came to you. Someone put a hit on me."

I let him absorb this. I can see his eyes widen a bit as he calculates the ever-shifting leverage between us.

"What's Ryan thinking?"

"Ryan's dead."

"Shiiiiiit." He lets this out low in his throat, like a growl. "So you want to know. . . ."

"I want to know who put the paper on me."

"Right. Right." He rubs his chin theatrically, like he's really stewing over the issue here, trying to figure out how he can help me. Archibald is the type who made gains all his life by convincing people he's stupid.

Finally, he nods. "Well, this is gonna take me a few days."

I stand. "Then I'll see you in a few days."

"You come to my office on Friday. I'll shake the trees and see what falls."

"Okay."

"You want the address?"

"I'll find you."

I can feel his eyes on me as I exit the room.

I lie low until Friday. My mind keeps turning back to Risina, and that story I told her, the one about the boy in the silver wagon, the kid looking down at his dead father, the kid who didn't know his name. When the walls start to close in on me I venture out from my hotel room to visit the Art Institute. I find myself standing in front of Magritte's painting of a locomotive racing out of a fireplace, smoke billowing out of its smokestack as a clock on the mantle above it points to nine. I can feel that wave rising over me as I stare at it, transfixed. The juxtaposition of those disparate images hits close to home to a hired killer standing amongst tourists and students and art lovers in the quiet starkness of the museum.

They think I'm just another patron, no different than them, in their world. They better hope their own clocks never strike nine.

I arrive at Archibald's office on Harrison, a former factory that must have manufactured an array of piping, based on the uncut aluminum lying around and the smell of stale air.

Six dead-eyed security guards stand sentinel, eyeing me as I approach. I don't have to say who I am, they know, they've been told, and they step aside as one shows me in to see the boss.

His demeanor has changed. I was afraid of this, was resigned to it, but I guess I had hoped he still had a residual fear of me and was eager to stay in my good graces. But Archibald Grant, above all else, is an opportunist.

"Here's the what-for. . . ." he says as soon as I sit down. "You ever see that movie *The Replacement Killers?*"

I shake my head.

"Jet Li? Directed by a black guy?"

I shake my head a second time.

"Well, you should check it out, Columbus. Rent it on Netflix. You know, when the shit settles. Anyway, I got ears all over, including all the way over on the other side of the Atlantic. Here's what you got staring at you down the other end of the barrel.

"Three killers. An Irish Setter named Leary what's got a beard and carries a blade."

"He's dead."

"Yeah, that's what I heard. Took two pops down in Georgia."

"You heard right."

"I told you I got ears. Here's where the replacement killers come in . . . one didn't do the job so your enemy hired two more."

"Hydra-style."

"Yeah, hydra-style, that's good. Anyway, you got a man out of

Czech Republic goes by the name of Svoboda . . . which I heard half the country goes by the name of. He's supposed to be a silver bear like you. Top, top, top shelf and then the shelf above that. I tried to get him in for a job once, but his fence just scoffed at me. So he must be collecting a pretty penny on you.

"And if that weren't enough ketchup on your hot dog, the other killer is an Argentine woman named Llanos. Don't ask me what that name means, cuz I don't know shit. I do know this woman executed some serious blood contracts down in South America. Her rep is that she's like morning frost . . . cold as ice and disappears when the sun comes up."

"Maybe I'll get lucky and they can pick off each other before they get to me."

"It's been known to happen."

"Yeah, well . . . I'll have to plan for the opposite."

"Yeah."

He leans back in his chair and laces his fingers behind his head. "Now we get down to the flop, turn and river and get all the cards out on the table."

"Lay 'em down for me then."

"You kill these two, four more coming. You know it and I know it. This big Papi wants you dead and he's got the bank account to make it happen, no matter how long you run. What you need to do is get to the source."

No, Archibald Grant may be a lot of things, but he isn't stupid. He's setting up a new proposition; his body language is as easy to read as a map. He's got all the pieces out on his chessboard, and he's preparing to mount an attack.

"I know who it is. I know the owner of the purse strings. I know who put the paper on you."

His fingers stay laced, and a grin spreads out on his face. I can barely look at all those teeth. I'm not going to help him along any further, so I hold my tongue.

"I'll give you the name too. I owe you that. For what happened to you and your fence on that Abe Mann job. It's just that I need you to do a little something for me first."

"Oh, yeah?"

"Yeah . . . nothing you can't handle straightaway."

"What is it?"

"A local job."

I shake my head. "Out of the question."

"Now look here. I need this. It's personal. I moved into Chi-town and there's a pair of pests I haven't quite scattered out of the kitchen. I worked up a file on em, but I don't want to use any of my guys. Best to look like these bucks made enemies elsewhere. That's where you come in. You can make it happen, cap'n."

"How about I *make* you tell me the name and then we never see each other again?"

He hasn't knocked that smile off his face. I imagine he has some hole card he wants to play; I might as well get it out on the table too so we both can see it.

"Well, see, let's not get hasty here. We're businessmen doing busi-ness. I went the extra mile for you, getting information you need to survive, and now I want something *from* you. And here's the kicker, Columbus . . . I'm the only one in the entire world who knows you took out Abe Mann right before the Democratic National Convention. You think that case file ain't still drawing teams of Feds and half the local departments in this country? You a smart guy . . . hell, maybe the best gun in the world. Fuck if I know. But I gotta take care of mine, and if I put a file in a safety box somewhere that outlines what I know, only to be released to the Federal authorities in the event of my untimely death, can you blame me?"

I start to say something, but he interrupts, still smiling. "And before you start talking about my family or my wives or my nieces and nephews or my grandpappy back in Georgia, just know that I don't give a South Side fuck about none of em. Knock yourself out. The only person on the Earth I care about is the one talking to you right now, and I'd say it's in your best interest to keep me alive."

He's got me and he knows it. There's nothing I can do but play along.

"I eighty-six your rivals, you give me the name?"

"We'll be all square."

"Then give me the goddamn file."

He leans forward in his chair, and I didn't think it was possible, but his smile grows even wider.

CHAPTER SEVEN

THE NAMES AT THE TOP OF THE PAGE ARE DALAN AND DARIUS WEBB. The attached pictures reveal a set of identical twins, black men in their late thirties. Sharp blue eyes contrast with dark skin and malevolent expressions. At first blush, they look like mirror images, but a closer inspection reveals Darius's nose as slightly longer, his jaw slightly sharper. Archibald's work in the file is meticulous and exact, like he relished the chance of putting this one together.

The Webb brothers like to keep to themselves, only venturing out of the condo they share near Lake Michigan when they have a meeting, either with one of their hit men or with a prospective client. Their unit sits on top of a well-guarded building, a place where people with a lot of money pay a hefty mortgage to keep those without a lot of money at bay. The dearth of firsthand information about their condo leads me to believe Archibald never penetrated it.

I've often struck people at their residences. The advantage the target holds in terms of knowing the location is countered by the simple fact that most people relax at home, let their guard down once the front door is locked. But the Webb brothers' choice of living quarters suggests their defenses are always engaged. Deliveries are halted at the door. Strangers are turned away. The only people allowed to enter the elevator have to be accompanied by a resident. No exceptions. Inconvenience has been traded for safety, with no regrets.

Archibald's file moves on to describe the brothers' operation. They have a roster of eight to ten gunmen whom they employ regularly, small-time guys who mostly work right here in Chicago. The Webb brothers are characteristic of the seedier side of the killing business, the cheap alternative to what I do, the 2-for-1 coupon in the back of the Shopper's Guide. They don't charge much, they take any job that comes their way, and they send as many guys as necessary to get the work done, no matter how sloppy. There's a market for low-rent killing, and these guys fill it.

My first fence taught me that to kill as I do, to execute a contract on someone's life and then walk away from it cleanly, I needed to *realize* a connection with the target so I could *sever* that connection. I needed to find aspects of my target's life I could hate, not just tangentially, but physically, viscerally *hate*, not just the noun "hate," but the verb "to hate," actively *hate*, with passion and concentration and emotion behind it. Only then could I kill, could I snap that connection, before moving on to the next target.

The Webb brothers are easy men to loathe. They take the art of my business and make it base and common. They have no respect for the profession. I can see it in the somnolent eyes staring out at me from the picture attached to the file.

They work out of the Union Stock Yards, what used to be the capital of the butchering industry in America, where Upton Sinclair famously focused his unblinking prose. Now heavily industrial, the only butchering ordered here appears to be of the human variety.

Their base is a renovated warehouse on Pershing Road. It is well armed and well guarded. Archibald has been inside, must have been when he first came to town and the brothers failed to realize they were meeting with a rival. His sketches of the layout are detailed, precise. They have three rooms, dimly lit, windowless. An office for each brother adjoins a conference room where they hand out assignments, meet with clients, put their files together. They have one permanent employee, a secretary named Craig Juda, a former Israeli soldier who files more than paperwork. Archibald spends a great deal of ink on Juda: his schedule, his history. He poses the biggest threat to making a clean hit. I'll avoid him if possible, kill him if necessary.

The trick to working a double, like this assignment, is to kill both marks within moments of each other. If I manage to kill one but not the other, I risk the target turning into a serious threat, fueled by anger and revenge and adrenaline. Or worse, the target goes underground, into deep hiding, off the page from whatever information my fence is able to put together ahead of time.

The best bet is to drop Dalan and Darius before either twin can process what befell the other.

Archibald Grant and I sit in the Golden Bull restaurant, a Chinese food dive near the Lakeside Hospital. After dropping off our food, the waitress moves over to a corner to take a nap. It's my kind of place.

"I hear what-tell the South American chick? Llanos? She's here in Chicago. Right now."

"How do you know?"

"That's my business."

"You running a play on me?"

"I'm *telling* you, man. I'm trying to help you." He doesn't meet my eyes, just digs his fork into his rice bowl. This is worrisome, though not entirely out of Archibald Grant's character. He's as shifty as desert sand, and I have a nagging feeling I made an error seeking him out.

"You got a leak in your office then. No one knows I'm here."

"Someone do. If that leak came from my office, there's gonna be blood on the floor by the end of the day, I guarantee you that."

I don't respond, and he keeps shoveling chicken and rice into his mouth, his fork scraping the side of the bowl.

Finally, he looks up, clearing his gums with his tongue. "How's the other thing shaking?"

"It's going to go down in a matter of days, maybe sooner in light of what you just told me. Make yourself available immediately after with the name I want on the tip of your tongue."

He leans back and flashes me that smile. "After all I do for you, you still don't trust me?"

"Thanks for lunch," I say, pushing my chair back.

"You gonna get 'em through the mother?"

I don't answer as I leave the restaurant.

I need to do this now, today. If someone leaked to Llanos my location in the windy city, then Svoboda can't be far behind. Who knows if they've already spotted me? Who knows if Archibald called that lunch meeting so they could start tracking me? Maybe they negotiated a deal with him. He points me out like Judas in the garden by sitting with me in the restaurant, and they pledge to descend upon me once I've taken out his rivals. It would be a dumb play on Archibald's part: either assassin will kill me as soon as he or she can, regardless of the promises they proffer to a small-time Chicago fence. Like I said before, Archibald is no imbecile. No, my gut says he was telling me the truth in order to warn me, that he wants my work finished and his rivals in body bags. After I complete the mission, well, that's another story. After I kill the Webb brothers, all bets are off.

He's right, of course. I'm going to get to them through their mother.

Her name is Laverne Contessa Webb and she lives alone in a home north of the city, in Evanston, near the Northwestern campus. She is the secret the Webb brothers have kept hidden since the moment they entered this line of work. They invented a biography for themselves, concocting an origin story out of the Western district of Baltimore: orphaned twins, victims of the drug wars of the early eighties.

They can talk a good game. They know the names of streets and row houses and corner boys and dealers from Baltimore in case someone has a cousin or a nephew from that part of the country and checks up on them. They know intimate details of major drug events from the past, when and where they were standing when Big Randy bought two to the head on Fayette Street, where and when they were standing when Tej Junior took over the corners on West Lombard. And yet, none of this history is true.

Dalan and Darius Webb grew up in Vancouver, Canada, the sons of a Methodist preacher. The preacher had a small congregation, a decent salary, a modest home, and a doting wife who loved him unconditionally. The preacher's wife, however, was not their mother.

Laverne Contessa Webb managed the office of the small church, serving at once as its accountant, secretary, social planner, fundraiser, and any of hundreds of other functions including, on occasion, sermon author. She worked closely with the preacher and fell for him when his mild flirtations gave way to serious advances. Once she became pregnant, she was chased from the church by a congregation who liked to listen to ancient stories about forgiveness while avoiding any themselves. The preacher rebuked her mercilessly as sin incarnate.

She fled to her childhood home, a small farmhouse in Iowa, where she and her elderly parents raised the twin boys. They were home-schooled, they worked on the farm, and they grew up with innate distrust. And when they chose this life, the killing life, they held on to only one thing from their sordid past: the love of their mother.

Damn, Archibald is full of surprises. That kind of backstory can take months, maybe years, to cobble together, especially since the marks worked very hard to concoct their own version of the past. But Archibald had discovered it all, laid it out in the pages of his report like a true crime novelist. And as much as I want to put a slug in the man's head for the aggravation he's causing me, I keep finding things to admire about him.

Laverne answers the door wearing a shawl around her thin shoulders. She is slender and frail; she's lost weight since Archibald managed to capture a few photos of her, like she's been fighting an illness and a strong gust of wind might blow her away.

"Ms. Webb?"

"Yes?"

"You . . . uh . . . you don't know me, but I've driven a long way to find you."

She raises her eyebrows and sticks out her lower lip, taking me in. "Oh?"

"I'm from Vancouver, ma'am."

She stiffens at the name of the city, and I press forward. "My father recently passed away."

"I don't understand what. . . ."

"Before he went, he asked that I find you, get in touch with you. It took me a long time, but I put the pieces together. Do you mind if I come in?"

I can tell she is thinking about it. "Would you mind telling me what this is about?"

"I'd rather do it inside."

She folds her arms.

I force an embarrassed smile on my face. "My father was a deacon at the King's Cross Methodist Church there in Vancouver, and he wrote a letter he wanted me to share with you. He said it was very important I give it to you. I think he's looking for some kind of absolution."

Her eyes move from my face to some point in the distance, like she's trying to see through to the past. Slowly, she nods. "All right, then."

"Thank you."

She steps aside and allows me to pass into the house, a mistake she will soon regret.

She is doing fine. Scared, yes, but doing as I ask as best she can under the circumstances. The cordless phone is up to her ear, and she watches me fearfully. Her eyes flit to the Glock resting comfortably in my right hand.

After a moment, one of her sons answers the line.

"Yo."

"Darius?"

His voice warms immediately. I guess I'm a little surprised she's able to distinguish between her two sons after hearing one syllable, but never underestimate a mother, I suppose. "Hey, Mom. How you doing?"

"Not so well."

"What is it?"

Before she can answer, I snatch the phone out of her hand and affect a gangland accent. "Bring me some money, yo." And then I hang up. And wait.

Juda, the bodyguard, is the first one through the door. Darius is right behind him, gathering steam as he barrels into the foyer. Both men have guns out and up in broad daylight, dismissing any worries of nosy neighbors watching them.

Dalan, the younger of the two twins by exactly seven minutes, hangs back by the car, double-fisting a pair of chrome .45 automatic Colts, high-caliber, knock-out punch guns. I'm sure he's there to ambush anybody foolish enough to try to escape out the front door.

My first shot hits him flush in the forehead while my second catches him under the chin as he drops. I didn't use a silencer, purposefully making as much noise as I can. The sound of the gunfire initiates the intended effect, Darius screams a guttural, maniacal wail as he bursts back out of the front door and races to the body of his twin brother, slumped backward against the rear tire of their Navigator, a lure too shiny to resist.

My third shot rips through the back of Darius's head, sending half of his skull into his dead brother's face.

Juda, standing halfway between the front door and the car, spins and looks at me where I lie on top of Laverne's roof. My gun points directly at him, a sure shot, a clean kill if I pull my index finger toward me an inch. I don't want to kill Juda, though. Not unless he does something stupid. As I mentioned before, I've found trouble can grow exponentially if I leave more of a mess than necessary, and bodyguards are always more interested in a paycheck than revenge.

He doesn't take his eyes off me. He's a true professional, a man who has seen his share of bodies, and he knows he's dealing with a killer who has the advantage. Slowly, he drops his guns and backs away, backs away, backs away, until he reaches the sidewalk. Then he turns and starts running, a sprinter, a man with nothing but monetary ties to the brothers and a will to live.

In a few moments, I am off the roof, leaping into the back yard and sprinting in the opposite direction, to my rental car parked on a neighboring street. I tied Laverne Webb to a chair in her kitchen, and I don't want to be within five miles of her house when she frees herself and comes looking for me. What I won't do is underestimate the mother.

CHAPTER EIGHT

I AM SITTING NEXT TO ARCHIBALD GRANT'S BED WHEN
HE TURNS ON HIS LIGHT. He doesn't flinch, just sits up and
props himself against the headboard. He is growing accustomed to
having me in his life.

"I might've been with a lady."

"You aren't."

"But I might've been. And you would've scared the insides out of
her, creeping up in here like that."

I shrug. "The job is done."

"The brothers are planted?"

"Head shots. Both of them."

Archibald smiles, all teeth. "Well, all right. You can wake me up for that kind of news any day of the week."

"Give me my name, and I'm on my way."

"Yeah, yeah. We had a deal and you came through true blue. Open up that drawer in the bedside table there."

Inside is a black notepad, the kind with a wire coil on top. I pass it to him.

"Hand me my glasses there."

I do, and he sets an old pair of bifocals on his nose, then starts flipping through the notebook, muttering to himself. "All right. Uh huh." He makes nodding motions with his head as he continues to flip. Finally, he stops on one page. "Here it is. The name you're look-ing for. Les'see, it's: Alexander Cole-Frett. Not sure how to pro-nounce that. Here, take the page."

He rips it out and I look at the name. *Alexander Coulfret* in block capital letters. The name looks familiar, but I can't peg it.

"That's all I have, Columbus. But he's the guy putting his signa-ture across the contract on your life. I know *that*."

"You have any idea why?"

"Can't say I do." He shrugs, feigning ignorance, his porcupine quills, his tortoise shell, his built-in defense.

I fold the paper away and stand.

Archibald takes off his glasses and folds his hands behind his head. "Say, this been a pleasure for me, working with you. I mean that. We should do it more often."

"Good luck, Archibald." I'm already moving toward the bedroom door.

"Columbus?" He waits for me to turn. "Don't tell no one about my glasses."

I can't help but smile. He scoots back down, rests his head against the pillow, and closes his eyes.

Coulfret. Coulfret. Where have I heard that name? It's French; I'm on the right track, but I've studied Noel's business dealings and his family tree going back generations and that name isn't there. And yet I know I've seen it. I know it.

I am sitting in the Hall public library on South Michigan, just about to type Coulfret's name into a Google window when the first bullet rips through my side. It's a low-caliber round but goddamn does it hurt, like someone swung a hammer into my rib cage.

A civilian's natural reaction is to drop to the ground when struck by a bullet no matter where it hits the body. It is ingrained from watching thousands of cop shows, thousands of movies, countless hours playing good guys and bad guys: when a gun goes off, the victim clutches his or her heart and falls to the earth like a punch-drunk prize fighter. But a professional killer knows better, knows you can live a long time with a .22 bullet inside you, knows that instead of dropping to the ground, you should be moving away from the direction the bullet hit your body.

I wasn't expecting this, had no warning other than the small cracking sound to my right followed by the blow to my side, but my instincts take over and people are starting to scream and flee and I act like I'm going to fall, only to leap onto the computer table, just as another crack and a bullet rips into the ground where the person holding the weapon thought I would drop, but I'm up and off the table and diving for a row between two bookshelves.

I catch a glimpse of some dark hair, and I know it's Llanos, the one from Argentina, and she managed to get one bullet in me but I'll be damned if she's going to manage two.

I chose poorly on the row; there are nothing but bookshelves and a concrete wall in front of me, so I swing low and dive through the "H"s in the biography section, scattering hard-covers like buckshot, until I burst out on the other side of the shelf, hitting the ground hard.

My ribs now feel like someone is trying to rip them out of my skin and I'm fighting to breathe, holding my shirt tight over the wound, but I'm pretty sure the bullet caught bone and stayed there, didn't ricochet, because I'm not throwing up blood, not yet, and my wits are still about me. I may not have anything else, but I've got that.

My eyes sweep my new position, homing in on the exits, because one thing is sure, a woman shooting a man in the middle of a Chicago public library is going to draw a hell of a lot of police. She knows it too and that may be my only advantage. She simply doesn't have time to try and finish the job, not if she wants to escape.

Across the aisle, I spot a door marked "Employees Only" and it's my best shot, my only shot, a break room or a snack room or something leading down or up or outside.

I grab a large book with the hand not pressed to my side, Lincoln's face on the cover, and fling it across the open aisle, no-man's-land, and I am moving while the book is still in the air. Lincoln draws the bullet instead of me and before a second shot is fired, I cross the ten steps to the employees' door, and I'm through it, startling a corpulent woman in a small hallway who smells like cigarettes.

"Smoking section!" I shout, a little louder than I would have liked, making the universal sign for cigarettes with the first two fingers of my good hand pressed to my lips and she's too surprised to do anything but point a chubby finger at a door at the end of the hallway.

Twenty yards and I'm slamming through the opening into sunshine and fresh air and freedom. My side feels like someone is jamming a spear into it; my right hand looks like I dipped it in paint.

The alley behind the library opens to the street and I spot a cab idling at the curb with a skinny white kid behind the wheel.

"Out now!" I scream as I fling open his driver's door, and in my periphery I see Llanos streaking around the corner, gun out and up. The woman has sand, I'll give her that.

The driver unbuckles his belt as he puts his hands up but he isn't moving fast enough. I yank him the rest of the way out of his seat, on to the sidewalk, and just as another volley of bullets pelts the side of the cab, I slide behind the wheel, throw the car in drive, and jam the pedal through the floorboard, not bothering to close the door. I couldn't if I wanted to, my left arm is pinned to my side; my right guides the wheel. It slams shut from the momentum as the car races forward.

I don't have much time. My vision is already going hazy at the edges, like I've stumbled into a tunnel. I need to think of something. Anything.

A quick glance in the rearview mirror, and goddammit, this Llanos woman is tenacious. I see her commandeer a second cab much as I took the first, and it roars away from the curb like a lion tracking wounded prey. She knows she landed a blow, and like a prizefighter crowding an opponent into the ropes, she'll be damned if she'll give up that advantage.

I throw the car around a corner, blinking doublevision out of my eyes, and if I'm going to do something, I'm going to have to do it now. My hold on consciousness is slippery at best, and the pain in my side is burning, like half my body has been lit on fire.

Before she can take the corner, I slam on my brakes, smoking the tires and just as quickly, I throw the stick into reverse and mash the pedal.

When killing a mark, there is only one sure way to put the target down permanently: a headshot. With a car, the principle holds, and any time you can sacrifice your trunk for your opponent's engine, you should launch at the chance.

I can't turn around, so I utilize the rear view mirror and grit my teeth and hope, hope, hope I'm timing this right and just as she blitzes around the corner, I thunder into her in reverse with a full head of steam.

Her hood crumples like an accordion, bucking the yellow cab up so the back tires threaten to flip over the front. Then the rear tires slam back to the pavement before her entire cab spins to the side.

I spin too, but am still facing away from her, thank God, and my engine is humming softly, so I shift back into drive and plow forward. My left rear tire is airless but the axle feels like it has kept its alignment and this poor cab may not get me far, but it should be enough. I eye the sideview mirror; Llanos's car remains in the middle of the street, smoke rising from its hood like a funeral pyre and if she makes it out before the whole thing goes up, at least it'll be with her confidence rattled. At least I gained that.

Now that my adrenaline is in full retreat, I feel tired, so damn tired, like I'm trying to walk along the bottom of the ocean. I need to make a move, a decision. I can't get much further limping in this cab. I have to find help. Goddamn, I need a fence. I have to....

Squash. Butternut squash soup, to be more specific, drips on my tongue and hits the back of my throat. I can smell it full in my nostrils, warm and salty. It might as well be a bone-in rib-eye. It tastes like the most delicious morsel I've ever put in my mouth.

I open my eyes and am staring at a young black woman, pretty, unthreatening. She is ladling the soup into my mouth with one hand under the spoon to keep it from dripping on to my chest.

"Hello." Her voice is warm, barely hiding a southern accent.

"Hello."

"How you feeling?"

"Stiff."

"You had a twenty-two slug in you, lodged into your rib. You want to see it?"

"No, thank you." She spoons another bite into my mouth and I can feel the heat moving down the length of my chest after I swallow.

"Just a second." She sets the bowl down and bounces over to a nearby door so she can stick her head into the hallway. She isn't dressed like a nurse or a caregiver; she's wearing a tight skirt and a half-shirt that shows off a belly ring.

"Archie! He's up!"

So I made it here after all. I remember throwing that Lincoln book—thanks for drawing another bullet, Mr. President—and I have images of a fat finger pointing me toward daylight and a cab barreling in reverse—but everything else bleeds together like Polaroids shuffled in a deck. I wanted to make it to a pharmacy and get the things I needed but I was slipping in and out of consciousness and didn't have a choice. I thought about Archibald and I must've made that decision but I don't remember doing so. I have no idea if I drove, walked, or crawled here. I'm vulnerable now, and I'm indebted to a man who knows how to exploit vulnerability, but I'm not sure I had another choice.

My side is throbbing, but what really bothers me, what my mind keeps turning over and over as it blocks out the pain is the play Llanos made. Archibald had warned me she had picked up my scent in Chicago, and so I went to a public library with a perfect view of my surroundings. Yet, she still took her shot there, even though her chances of finishing the job were limited. Then she kept after me, long past time when she should've retreated. The only reason she would do that, I imagine, is the third assassin, the Czech named Svoboda, is also here. She wanted to collect the kill fee before him, or she was worried he'd come after her first. Either way, she tried to force a low-percentage play. I'm going to make that decision come back to haunt her.

Archibald pokes his head in the room and I have to squint from the glare off all those teeth.

"Back from the abyss." His voice is as bouncy as the girl's step. "I must say I thought it'd be a while before you knocked on my door again. I guess something up in the universe got us tied together on the same string."

"Thanks for the patch-work."

"I got a surgeon who likes cash money and doesn't like paying malpractice. We got what the Nature Channel calls a symbiotic relationship."

"You got a mirror?"

"This face? I got a house full of 'em."

He moves off and the girl smiles at me. "Archie tells me you're the best he ever worked with."

"Archibald talks too much."

"Been that way since we were five. He had half our school working for him. The teachers too. Only one he couldn't keep up with was our mother."

"I'd like to have met her . . . just to complete the picture."

Archibald steps back into the room, holding a hand mirror. "That old lady taught me everything I know."

"She'd roll over in the grave to hear that."

So Archibald—Archie—has a sister and he thinks we're square enough to let me in on that secret, even after I got to the Webb brothers through their mother. It's a calculated move on his part. I showed up at his place completely helpless, exposed and dying; in return, he exposes himself, personally, to me, tying us even tighter together. Maybe the universe really does have us dangling on the same string.

I take the mirror and hold it at an angle to get a look at the wound in my side. Peeling the gauze and bandage back, I'm impressed with Archibald's surgeon. The wound is clean and the stitches are tight and even.

"I told you," Archibald says from the door.

"Yeah, pretty good." The pain is awful now, throbbing in time with my heartbeat. I don't want to know what it's going to feel like if I cough.

"You need some Tylenol or something?" the sister asks.

"I'll take some if you got 'em."

"Not a problem." She turns to go, then stops. "I'm Ruby, by the way."

"Columbus."

"I know who you are."

I've got a laptop in bed with me, and I'm chasing down the name Alexander Coulfret. Nothing on Google except an article from 2003 listing the victims of a Paris bus crash. An Alex Coulfret is among the dead, the tragedy taking place when a train leaving the city sideswiped a stranded bus. Nothing else. One mention of a dead guy and that's it. Whoever he is, he's kept his name blank in a world where most names are a keyboard click away. Maybe Archibald misspelled it.

I try typing in just the name "Coulfret" and I'll be damned. Fourteen articles from various European papers pop up, all focused on one particular incident, the murder of capitalist Anton Noel in the middle of Paris. I swallow, knowing I've found the right set of keys. Now, which one fits into the lock?

I click on the first article, the one I read in *Le Monde* while waiting in the train station in Naples before Ryan died giving me his warning. I scan it quickly, searching, searching . . . nothing leaps out at me and then I see it: Jerome Coulfret. A forty-five-year-old jeweler. One of two unfortunate civilians struck down when Noel's car flipped in a Paris intersection just as they were crossing it on foot. An innocent guy, cursed with black luck, caught in the wrong place at the wrong time. The confrontation in the bait-and-tackle store, the shot in the library, the bullet removed from my side, they had very little to do with Anton Noel after all. It was my sloppiness, my improvisation, my botched job that led to Jerome Coulfret's accidental death. Like I said, trouble grows exponentially when you leave more of a mess than necessary.

I'm guessing Jerome has a brother who might be a bit unhappy with the way my assignment to kill Noel went down.

I'm getting dressed when Archibald comes in and leans against the doorframe.

"Three weeks here. I was just about to ask you to get the fuck out."

I smile. How the hell this guy grew on me, I have no idea, but he has. I can't laugh, though, not with my ribs feeling the way they do.

"I gotta get back before the noose gets any tighter. End this thing."

"You don't have to tell me. You think I want two top-shelf killers figuring out I'm the one played Florence Nightingale with you? Or get on this Cole-Frett's shit list? They might start thinking I'd know how to find you and want a word with me. I'll pass on that, thank you very much."

I finish and reach for my pair of Glocks. "You cleaned these for me. You thoughtful bastard."

"Not me," Archibald says, raising his palms as he backs out the door. "I'd say good-bye, but something tells me I'm going to see you again." He's down the hall by the time I emerge from the room.

Well, I have to give him a tip of the cap. I thought he'd try to lord this over me, ask me to pay off my new debt to him by shouldering some other difficult assignment. At the very least I thought he'd ask me to join him, partner with him, the same way William Ryan did after my first fence, Pooley, died. But if he wants something from me, he's saving it for later. I wonder how long it'll be before I hear the front doorbell jingling on that one.

When I get to the door, Ruby is there, blowing on a warm cup of coffee.

"Back to the shooting business. . . ." she offers, her eyes merry.

"I'm just trying to keep the shooting business off me right now."

"So I heard."

"Archibald tells you a lot."

"Who do you think handles most of his contracts?"

I'll admit, I didn't see that coming. Family members often work together on the business side of the game. But this is the first time I've encountered a brother and sister who are also fence and assassin. The Grants grow more interesting by the minute.

"You're a bagman?"

"I know a little about a little."

"Well, now I know who cleaned my guns."

"You noticed."

"Yes. And thank you."

"Don't mention it, Columbus. If I'm ever shot in the ribs in Europe, I'll know who to come find."

"You'll have to find me first."

"That's the idea."

"See you around."

"I hope so."

She takes another sip of coffee and heads back toward the kitchen.

CHAPTER NINE

I HAVE TWO STOPS TO MAKE BEFORE I BEGIN TO HUNT ALEXANDER COULFRET IN FRANCE.

First, I need to visit my home in Positano. I realize this is pregnant with danger—the worst mistake a man with a price on his head can make is to walk through his own front door. But I'm growing weary of looking over my shoulder, and I need to load up on supplies and check to see if my residence has, in fact, been compromised.

The second stop involves Rome and a woman with a meaningless name who I can't get off my mind.

Positano is built into the side of a cliff, and I fell in love with it the moment I arrived here to kill a man named Cortino many years ago. When I needed a place to live abroad, it called to me just as Risina described Italy calling to her. I too found it difficult not to answer.

I bought a modest house about halfway up the hill and used it sparingly, so the locals would think of it as my second home. The long-time residents of Positano are as insular as the city itself, and I utilize their natural distrust of "summer people" to avoid forging relationships.

The sky and the sea are almost the exact same shade of color as I drive into the city on a motorcycle. I have spent my adult life blending into the background of every environment: dressing myself, carrying myself and expressing myself in ways that are the opposite of eye-catching. The motorcycle I drive is old and rusty and unmemorable, the same as a hundred bikes swarming the Italian countryside at the moment.

I park the bike near the beach, a twenty-minute walk from my front door, and start the climb. From my vantage point below, I can see the outside of my house, a beige two-story manor, perched on the side of the cliff. It looks undisturbed, and I'm not sure if that is a relief or a cause to be nervous. At least if I could pinpoint something unusual—a window shade up, broken glass—I could proceed with a plan. I have no choice but to be acutely cautious.

As a killer, I train myself to map out escape routes, no matter where I am or what I am doing. I do it without thinking, as natural and involuntary as exhaling. When I bought this house—Ryan actually did the buying, through a third party—I immediately set about renovating it, alone. The killing profession teaches you many useful disciplines; a basic knowledge of carpentry can be indispensable in a number of ways. I didn't upgrade the fixtures in the kitchen or expand the closets in the master bedroom. The upgrades I managed were for one purpose: getting into and out of the house without being seen.

I ascend stone steps laid out for homeowners and adventurous tourists, climb half of the hill, and then break from the main path when I am assuredly alone. The pain from the wound in my side has diminished, but not completely. It throbs now, marking each step with a pinprick to my ribs. I have heard about people's ability to compartmentalize pain, to suppress it, put it down in a hole below the line of consciousness, but fuck if I've ever been able to do it. My ribs hurt, and the only thing that will get me back to feeling a hundred percent normal is time.

Along a smaller trail, I can approach my house from the side, and if I squeeze in next to the wall and a dense row of evergreen hedges, I remain invisible. Near the base of the wall is a crawlspace entry. Its only distinguishing mark is a thin beige rope. I can tell from its position that the rope is undisturbed, just as I left it. I use it to pull the cover free. Before I enter, I reach my hand inside, and from memory, punch a sequence into a small alarm I installed just above the opening. A tiny beep indicates the space has been uncompromised since I last left. I take a breath and push through into the darkness.

From here, I only have to crawl a few feet to an area where I can stand, and from there, I open a hidden entrance into a laundry room next to my kitchen. The room is silent and musty, like the air has been trapped in here for months, a good sign.

After twenty minutes and a thorough inspection of each room, I am convinced the house is clear and remains undiscovered. If Leary, the Irish assassin I dispatched in Georgia, had beaten the information out of Ryan, he didn't have a chance to follow up on it. If he has passed the knowledge of my residence to anyone else, they haven't come calling. Yet.

I own only a few pieces of furniture, a bed, and a closet full of dark T-shirts, dark jeans and shoes. I undress, take a shower with the water turned up just below scalding, redress my wound, and then wedge as many clothes into a duffel bag as I comfortably can. A false front in the closet gives way to my weapons stash, and I load a black backpack with pistols and ammunition and extra clips. Finished, I take a look around the house, and allow myself two minutes at the back window looking down the cliff face at the black sand and the gray sea. In my head, I'm already using the words "the" instead of "my." It's "the" house, not "my" house.

Twenty minutes later, I am straddling the motorcycle, my duffel in the storage compartment under the seat, my backpack secure on my back. This will be the last time I see Positano, and I feel a melancholy pang in my chest. It looks as it always has: quiet and proud. I turn my head, kick-start the engine, and motor away.

An assassin's life is marked by movement. Loiter too long in one place and you won't be pleased with what catches up to you.

I can guess what happened.

Risina's co-worker handed her a cryptic message when she arrived at work. "Anonymous man called. Has first edition Lewis and Clark, 1814. Must sell. Meet in St. George lobby. 9:00 P.M."

Risina must've smiled, curious, intrigued. She must've asked Alda to describe the man's voice, but Alda probably shrugged dismissively. The man had requested Risina specifically, that's all Alda knew. He was just a man on the phone, and he kept everything succinct.

Risina might have called around to see if other contacts in the rare-book world had caught wind of a first edition Lewis and Clark entering the market. The lack of confirmation probably piqued her curiosity.

She must've gone home and chosen a black suit to wear. Conservative, but feminine. A suit conveying that her occupation dealt on the intersection where business and creativity collide.

She must have then walked to the hotel, pleased her anonymous caller chose a place just a few blocks from her home. She had her financial ledger tucked in tight at her elbow, a check and a pen ready if the seller needed to make this deal happen immediately.

She had no idea a man was watching her from the moment she left her apartment. She had no idea the man was scouring the area like a hawk, looking for any hint of abnormality, any hint of a pursuer, any threat to himself. She had no idea that the man was heavily armed, that the man was a professional, that the man was dangerous.

She probably sat in the lobby of the St. George Hotel, growing anxious and annoyed with each passing minute. She probably wondered if she was the victim of a hoax or if Alda was losing her mind. At some point, she wandered into the library, just off the lobby.

Her beauty was electric, powerful. It drew eyes to her like a beacon cutting through fog. She was the opposite of the man. It almost hurt him to approach her.

"Hello, Risina."

She turns and her smile is broad and warm.

"Jack!"

"You're not going to be too upset if it's just me instead of Lewis and Clark?"

She crosses to me instantly and embraces me with her whole body. I can't remember the last time I held someone in my arms like that, without reservation.

"You are a bad man."

"I've told myself that many times."

"You could have just called me and told me you were in town."

"What would've been the fun in that?"

She hits me playfully and pulls back, smiling. Goddamn, she is beautiful.

"Did you get a room here?"

"Yes, but that's not what I—"

"Take me to it."

An hour later, we lie exposed on the sheets, her head on my chest, her fingers intertwined with mine.

"I can honestly say I thought about you each day you were gone." Her voice is low in her throat, like a cat's purr.

"I'm sorry I couldn't get back here sooner."

"How was business?"

"Ongoing."

Her lips form a moue. "Does that mean you'll be leaving soon?"

"Yes."

"This is how it's going to be, isn't it?"

"Just for now."

"Don't tell lies for my sake."

"I'm not. I've been thinking quite a bit about changing jobs."

"Oh?"

I stroke her hair, tracing her eyebrows with my thumb.

"Yes, finding something where I wouldn't have to move around so much."

"And you would settle in Rome?"

"Would you like that?"

"I like you, Jack. Very much. There is something inside me that tenses every time I see you. I don't know how to describe it, but it happens. It is something I look forward to . . . this feeling . . . and not knowing when I'm going to experience it again has been . . . difficult for me."

She takes her hand out of mine and sits up on her elbow so she can look at me. "I'm sorry. I'm not expressing myself well. The way I mean to."

"You're very pretty."

She frowns. If I can change the subject abruptly, so can she. "Tell me about your scars."

She looks down when she says this, like she's afraid of my response.

I knew it was coming . . . her fingers had traced my wounds earlier, and I winced once when we shifted places. But I'm not sure, even now, I'm not sure I'm ready to let her in. Once that door swings open, it is impossible to close.

She senses my hesitation and lies back down, resuming her position with her head on my chest. For a minute, I think she isn't going to speak again, that she may fall asleep right there. But I am wrong.

"A man paid for my education. In America."

I know she has more to say, so I wait.

"I was seventeen and worked in a small grocery store on the other side of Rome, near Vatican City. I worked there from the time I was thirteen, making a few lira after school so I could help my parents. The man who owned the store . . . his name was Giuseppe Rono. My parents and others in the neighborhood didn't like him, didn't trust him. He had moved into the neighborhood from a farming village near Siena. He was unmarried and had an ugly face.

"He would come to the gymnasium at the school and watch the girls play soccer, even though he had no daughter on the team. There were whispers—I heard them from my friend's parents, from neighbors—of how his eyes would linger too long on the girls running and jumping and playing. It was a time when people didn't talk about such things, and still, there was talk. My parents wanted me to quit working in his shop, but I refused. I was a strong-willed girl, and I was at an age when I would choose to do whatever my parents forbid. As the weeks progressed, Giuseppe Rono and I became friendly. I would stay after work to talk to him about the latest gossip from school and he would listen to it all, passing on advice and taking an interest in all my activities, always ready to lend his ear.

"One afternoon, he called me into the small office he owned

behind the store. He was seated behind a wooden desk, and his hand was down in his lap where I couldn't see it. His arm was moving slightly, and I could see he was sweating, even though it was cool that day. His face was smiling, but it was . . . I don't know how you say it in English . . . ?"

"Lopsided?"

"Yes, that's it. A lopsided smile. I remember thinking I was a fool, I had failed to heed everyone's warnings and they were right about Giuseppi Rono. I cursed him, though the words wouldn't come out. I hated him, though my face couldn't move. If I'd had a gun in my hand, I would've shot him right there. I know it.

"He wanted to show me something, he told me. I was paralyzed . . . I knew I should turn and run away but my legs wouldn't work, I couldn't make them work."

She takes a breath, gathering herself.

"Goddamn him, I thought. Damn him for betraying me like this. He started to stand up and I wanted to tear my eyes away but I couldn't avert them. I couldn't move, no matter how much my mind screamed at me to go, just go! Run away from that place screaming. . . .

"I looked down at his lap, and in his hands, he was holding a sheet of paper, folding it and refolding it nervously. 'Risina,' he told me, his face expectant, hopeful. 'Risina, I had a wife and child who died many years ago in an auto crash in Siena. My daughter, her name was Christiana, she would have been your age.' His voice was shaking, and he continued to turn that paper over and over. 'I have contacted the University in America, the one you told me you could not afford. I have set up an account for you, Risina. To pay for your schooling. It was money set aside for Christiana, but you have been the daughter she was to me. You must accept this, Risina. You must let me do this for you while I can. It would mean everything to a brokenhearted and lonely man.'

"I don't remember what happened after that . . . I remember hugging him so hard I thought he might break. I remember my parents coming into the office . . . he had already contacted them and explained his situation. They were ashamed, but proud. Proud of me and my chance for an education. I remember my father's hand pumping Mr. Rono's, and I remember the smile on Rono's face so large I thought it would light up the sun. And all I could think about as I hugged him, all I could think about was that I had rushed to hate him just ten minutes before. That I would have shot him with a gun if I'd had the chance. That I had cursed him.

"He died of cancer the month after I graduated. He was too sick to attend the ceremony, but he wrote me a letter which I carry with me always."

Her voice stops but the story remains between us like a tangible object.

I run my hand through her hair again, splay it out against my chest, unsure what to say. After a moment, she takes my fingers back in hers.

"I've learned there can be a great distance between perception and the truth. And I know there are things about you you wish to keep a mystery from me. Just know that I won't rush to judge you, Jack. The one thing I will never do is judge you."

The shower is therapeutic, and the pain in my side from the bullet wound has diminished to nothing more than a twinge. I feel better than I've felt in a long time, for as long as I can remember, actually.

I can see it now, like a map unfolded in front of me. There is an end to this, to this life. I can shed it like a snake's skin. Throughout adulthood, I've felt like this job defined me, was a part of me, was inside me. But I see it now, I can *see* it, goddammit, maybe for the first time.

I haven't left it, haven't escaped it, because I didn't *want* to leave this way of life. I never cared about the money; it was the challenge and the skill and the craft and the power I devoured like an addict. And after years of doing the job, of sharpening my abilities, of mastering my prowess, of forgetting Jake, the only woman who knew me as something other than a killer, I'd lost any measure of what my life could be without it.

But Risina changes that. Is she an ideal? Is my desperation for human contact coloring how I view the woman asleep in the bed outside this bathroom? Am I purposely turning a blind eye to her faults, creating in my mind a Madonna void of blemishes, when the truth must fall far short?

The answer is: I don't give a damn.

I am out of the shower, dried and dressed, tying my shoes when she stirs.

"You are leaving?"

"Yes. Take your time. Order breakfast to the room."

She sits up, unselfconsciously. I can't help but look at her, drinking her in. Like her laughter before, it is an image I know will sustain me over the next few weeks, as I finish this and free myself.

"Do you think you will be long this time?"

"I don't know. I don't think so. But I don't know."

"Is there danger you will not come back at all?"

"Why do you ask?"

"I know what those scars are, Jack. There's a bullet wound in your side. Old bullet wounds in your shoulder and on your chest. I can only imagine what made the other marks."

She says it matter-of-factly, with no malice in her eyes.

"I will be back. I promise."

"I believe you."

"I will tell you everything when I return."

"I believe that too."

I head for the door and reach for the handle.

"Jack. . . ."

"Yes?"

"Be sure and bring that first edition Lewis and Clark with you when you come back to me."

She is grinning and her eyes are merry.

"I will."

I pull the door behind me and walk away from the room, down the corridor, alone. My smile disappears by the time I reach the street.

CHAPTER TEN

ALEXANDER COULFRET IS GOING TO BE A DIFFICULT MAN TO KILL.

Without a fence, a middleman, to put a file together, I am learning the craft on my own. I have a new respect for the job Vespucci, Pooley, and Ryan did, the job Grant and Doriot still do. I suppose I could have phoned Archibald Grant in Chicago and seen what blanks he could fill in regarding Coulfret, but I just don't want that particular string tied any tighter. I already owe the man enough.

When I've needed information in the past, I've either stolen it from the shadows, or I've compelled someone to give it to me against his or her will. In those instances, the information I seek is specific—the location of a particular mark on that given day, say—and I don't have to worry about returning to the source again.

But compiling a background file on a man, a large dossier so I have myriad choices of how and where and when to strike, requires a much different approach.

I start in the offices of *Le Monde*, posing as an American film writer. My former fence Pooley once explained people will do anything to help you if they think there is an outside chance of being immortalized. People from all walks of life—waitresses to senators—would open up to him and spill their secrets as he appealed to their vanity, claiming to be a screenwriter, a reporter, a novelist, a film producer. I intimate I am researching a script centering on Parisian crime, a *French Connection* for the new millennium, and I need background information on a man named Alexander Coulfret.

A public relations woman escorts me to their catalog room, where every article, every scrap of paper, including reporter's notes in some instances, has been added to an enormous database. The woman, BeBe, is genial and coquettish. She sets me up in a cubicle, asks if I need anything to drink, hands me her card, and then leaves me alone with the computer.

Hours later, I emerge from the building with the following information.

A young man named Alex Coulfret was arrested twice in the nineties, once for robbery and once for stabbing a man with a knife, though the victim made a full recovery. Both articles mention jail time, but there is no followup reporting to indicate whether or not Alex was found guilty or whether he served. Both arrests occurred on the east side of the city, in the Eleventh arrondissement, near the

Bastille. Information about the perpetrator is scant, a "white male in his twenties" the full extent of the description.

Only one other occurrence of the name appears in the newspaper, a mention in the bottom of that article from 2003, the one I found when I first punched the name Alexander Coulfret into Google back in Archibald's apartment. I barely glanced at it before, but now I study the details a bit more closely. A train leaving Paris crashed into a stranded bus just outside the city, killing twelve people. Listed alphabetically among the dead: Alex Coulfret. The article is maddeningly short—no other details emerge about the victims—like it was written just before the evening deadline. I check the next day's edition and find no mention of the crash; the story was swept away by the bombings of the U.S. embassies in Tanzania and Kenya.

These buried facts are tiny seeds, just specks of information, but they start to grow into a portrait of the man who paid the contract on my life. First, I'm guessing he was born in or near the Bastille district; the connection between the two arrests indicates proximity, familiarity. Second, the types of offenses certainly keep in line with a low-level member of a criminal organization. Not every arrest makes the paper. I wonder how many more crimes Alex committed or was arrested for in his early adulthood. Third, a man who has the resources to hire a trio of professional killers also has the resources to fake his own death, to land his name on a list of the deceased following a fatal public accident. The short time—ten years between *Le Monde* mentions—gives me pause.

I've been in a position to observe the inner workings of organized crime many times. Most mafias operate similarly: loyalty is rewarded; men rise through the ranks by some combination of battle-tested fealty and unfettered nepotism. Usually, this process can take an entire lifetime, and even then, a man's stupidity or nerve can hinder him from rising past a low-level position within the enterprise. That Alex Coulfret ascended from armed stick-up man to a position powerful enough to fake his own death in such a relatively short time means my enemy is most likely intelligent, artful, and ruthless.

If I'm wrong, and the three mentions aren't as colorful as I'm suggesting, then it does me no harm to assume the man is formidable. But I don't think I'm wrong.

The next avenues I plan to investigate are the local police files on Coulfret. Perhaps they have more details tucked away in the back of a detective's cabinet than in the database of the newspaper. Maybe the police know all about the man and are actively hunting him now, as I am.

I call BeBe at *Le Monde* from a pay phone near the Bastille and enlist her help in introducing me to a friendly police detective in the eleventh district. She is more than happy to do so; she knows just the man with whom I should speak, a detective named Gerard. How soon would I like to get started?

I hang up after agreeing on a meeting point and walk toward that creperie. I notice a young boy who can't be more than six or seven, holding on to his father's hand, coming toward me on the sidewalk ahead. The boy has to take two steps just to match his father's pace, and the man never looks down at his child, lost in his own world. My mind turns to that silver wagon with the dropped handle. Why is that image so damned important to me? Why is it always on the edge of my mind, waiting like a stranger in the shadows, prepared to leap out and suffocate me at a moment's notice?

I think I know the answer, though I don't want to face it. Years ago, my father hired me to kill him, though I didn't know all the details until the end. I thought I had mentally closed that door, put it behind me, walled it off, but maybe it can never fully be closed. At one time I thought I had control over the past, could shut it off from my mind like turning off a faucet, but I was wrong. Maybe it will always be with me, breaking its valve and pouring out whenever I'm vulnerable. Maybe....

I catch a flash of silver ducking into a fabric shop across the street.

Something was off about it, something a little conspicuous, like a signal, and I cross the Rue Sedaine quickly, without thinking, reliant on years of heightened instinct. I know it'll be a problem ducking into an unfamiliar store and there will be a delay as my eyes adjust from light to dark, but my feet carry me on, almost involuntarily.

What did I see? A piece of clothing? The flash of sunlight reflecting off of a gun barrel? I was too entranced in watching that kid and his father and that silver handle in my head and now I'll have to grit my teeth and enter the place and if the Argentine woman wants to shoot me again then she should've pulled the trigger while my mind was on that boy who couldn't remember his name.

She didn't, though, and I'll rely on my intuition as I pop through the door and scan the room. The fabric shop is small; there's no one inside except an elderly Persian woman behind the cash register, but a carpeted stairwell with a sign pointing up reading "shawls" in

English looms next to her.

I have my Glock in my hand as I head up the stairwell, trying to keep my footfalls silent, but the noise is deafening in the oppressive quiet of the store.

An uneasy feeling tightens my throat and I can feel the short hairs on the back of my neck rising. I've made many mistakes since taking that file from Ryan outside the cathedral in Turin, but this takes the fucking cake, plodding up a narrow stairwell toward a dimly lit second floor with a possible assassin at the top. If I get shot, I'll go down pulling the trigger. If I get jumped, I'll go down swinging. I'm ascending the final step, and there is an armed woman up here, but not the one I thought.

"She's here."

Ruby Grant, Archibald's sister, stands next to a tiny window, peering down at the street. She nods for me to join her, and when I do, I catch a glimpse of another woman, this one with inky hair, stalking quickly down the sidewalk, searching, confused. I've seen her before, in a library in Chicago. The last time we met, I was ramming the back end of a yellow cab into the front end of hers.

Below, the woman breaks from our sight line and is gone.

Ruby appears amused, like she's in the middle of telling a brilliant joke.

"That's Llanos."

"Yeah. . . ."

"She got to Archie."

"Got to him?"

"Well, got to talk to him, I should say. Archie's good at talking. Always has been. He put her on your trail, then put me on hers."

"He's starting to rack up too many favors."

"He likes you."

I'm not sure how to respond to that, and Ruby sees it on my face. Her grin grows as effortlessly as an exhale, what must be a family trait.

"So you flew all the way here to warn me?"

"Don't go gettin' ideas. Professional preservation. At this point in the game, you being dead doesn't do my brother much good."

"What do you think me being alive does for him?"

Ruby shrugs. "Something I guess Archie will figure out at a later date."

She nods out the window. "So how you want to handle this?"

"I'm going to drop her. Quietly."

"I *know* that. I'm just asking if you want me to tag-team with you."

"No. I'm afraid I already owe your family too much for my own good."

"Suit yourself."

I turn to head back down, hurrying so I don't lose the trail of the woman who came here to kill me.

"Columbus. . . ."

I stop.

"See you soon."

I nod and clomp heavily down the stairs, afraid she's probably right.

Llanos is half a block in front of me, addled. She was good enough to pick up my trail without alerting me, but not good enough to keep from losing the scent when I zigged when she thought I would zag. One mistake. As is the case so often in what we do, one mistake is the difference between Llanos living through the day and never seeing tomorrow's sunrise.

She checks the street signs, watches the shadows, and I can see resignation manifest on her face. She lost me, even though she's not sure how. She retraces her steps, bewildered, and then hurries in a trot toward the Rue de Lappe and the crepe shop where my meeting with the police detective is supposed to take place. So she must've been listening in on my call or wrenched the information from the PR woman at the newspaper, BeBe. I hope it is the former.

If I am going to ambush her, it is best to do it now, before she reaches the creperie a few blocks away, before the officer I'm supposed to be meeting witnesses the shooting.

An ambush is all about information and timing. I know where she's headed, which allows me to dart over a block to the south, then up the street at a sprint, then over again to arrive in front of her. The timing centers on waiting until the final possible moment to take the first shot, to remove her defenses before she has a chance to engage them.

I stop at the corner, waiting for Llanos to materialize in front of me. She's as oblivious as a rat sniffing cheese attached to a metal spring. I estimate I have thirty seconds before she emerges. The street is mostly deserted, so I'm not concerned about witnesses; perhaps the driver of a passing car will see something, but usually the shock of violence, the cacophony of a gunshot, gives me the freedom to hustle away unnoticed from the scene.

A door opens next to me and a crowd starts to spill out on to the sidewalk, children and parents and grandparents, and it is some sort of celebration complete with balloons and streamers and laughing and singing and they are passing me, heading for the corner directly in front of me, the intersection of the Rue de la Roquette and the Passage Thieré where I plan to take Llanos's life.

She should be approaching any second now and she'll be surrounded by the crowd, but she won't be protected, and as I instantaneously form a new plan, my hand moves from the Glock inside my shoulder holster to the blade I keep near my waist.

The seconds slow and the world stops spinning and the children freeze in mid-smile as my senses warp like they've been jolted with electricity and Llanos steps out from the street into my view, and she's ignoring the festive families, looking straight ahead when she should be checking around every corner instead of hurrying to make the next block.

I cut through the crowd like a scythe and her periphery vision kicks in as I approach with the blade in my hand and she's a moment too late as I swing my arm in a fluid arc and the stiletto smashes into her throat at the precise point above where her windpipe disappears below her sternum.

I don't break stride, keep moving, cross the street and duck a right, heading for the little bastion that started a revolution. When she falls to her knees, clutching her throat, trying to keep the blood from spilling out through her fingers, when the first child screams and when the parents pull all the boys and girls and grandparents away, hoping they haven't seen too much, I will be gone.

CHAPTER ELEVEN

THE OFFICER SMILES WARMLY WHEN I GREET HIM, HALF STANDING BEHIND A WEDGE OF A TABLE IN THE MIDDLE OF THE CREPE SHOP AT THE END OF THE RUE DE LAPPE. He has ordered a croque monsieur, devoured the first triangle and is two bites into the second when I shake his hand.

"You are Mr. Walker, yes?"

"I am. Thanks so much for meeting me."

"It is my pleasure, my pleasure. Ms. Lerner tells me you are a writer?"

"Yes. . . ."

"Very pleased to meet you. My name is Gerard. I too write a little fiction. Nothing published as yet, but I am delighted to say a little printing press from Lyon has been in contact with me recently and has expressed interest in reading my next submission."

He is a round man, with wide shoulders and only a hint of a neck, constructed like a snowman. Somehow, he takes bites of his sandwich while maintaining the cadence of his speech, and words tumble out of him at the same time as his food disappears from his plate. It's fascinating to watch, like a magician with a rabbit, and I have a hard time paying attention to what he's saying.

"But they say writing is to write what you know and my occupation as an officer in Paris has led to many, many interesting stories, I can assure you, so let me, may I ask, what type of writing is it you do?"

"Well, a little bit of everything but mostly film writing."

He pats his heart affectionately, a theatrical swoon. "Ahh, it is my dream, yes? Hollywood, movies, your words on the silver screen, yes? And what is it you have written that I might know?"

"Well, nothing that's been produced as yet, but that's why I'm here. Hoping to collect more information about organized crime in Paris."

He winks, as happy as a child opening a present. "A *French Connection*, yes? That is what Ms. Lerner intimated to me, and I immediately said 'ah, yes' because you see I have been working on a crime story as well as I'm sure you can imagine. I hope you do not steal my story, no, ha, ha, I'm certain that there is plenty of crime to go around, certainly in Paris, yes?"

His radio squelches and I hear a burst of information in colloquial French about a stabbing but he moves his fat fingers down to his waist and quickly twists the knob to cut off the sound.

"Pssh, interruptions, interruptions, now let me tell you the story I am working on, yes, and then you can tell me how I may help you and maybe when I'm finished with my new manuscript you can sell the rights to Martin Scorcese for me, ha, ha, ha, yes?"

Without waiting for me to respond, he plunges into his tale of a put-upon French policeman in the Bastille district who is misunderstood because of his weight problem. He is the hero, you see, and much smarter than even his superiors care to admit. Twenty minutes later and Officer Gerard is finally concluding the narrative and somehow a croque madame has joined her husband in his stomach without the detective missing a single plot twist or stultifying morsel of dialogue.

When he finally reaches the end, breathless, I force on my most engaging smile and tell him I am certain my agent in Hollywood will want to read the novel as soon as it is finished. He laughs like I've told a hilarious joke, emits a greasy burp, and then shakes my hand without bothering to brush the crumbs from his shirt. "Maybe we will both be walking down the red carpet next year, yes, yes, ha ha."

Thirty minutes later, we are inside the conference room dedicated to Organized Crime within his department's headquarters, flipping through detailed files covering the last two decades.

It only takes a few more seconds of flattery before I am alone.

The first time Alex Coulfret officially came to the attention of the specialized branch of the French police was eight years ago. A new lieutenant named Chautier had been promoted within the Organized Crime department and was challenged with tightening a rope around the professional criminals moored in his district. He had been educated in New York and Washington and had returned to his native city with a different approach to tackling the problem, one that promoted sending a mix of uniformed and plainclothes police officers out onto the streets, not to make arrests or threaten incarceration, but simply to listen. A neighborhood is a living entity, Chautier preached: it sleeps, it eats, it breathes, and quite often, if you allow it a slight bit of freedom, it talks.

One name popped up on the lips of citizens again and again: Alexander Coulfret. From what the police officers could surmise after sifting through rumors and eyewitness accounts and exaggerations and embellishments, Coulfret had started as muscle for an aging boss named Dupris. He was used for everything from shakedowns to collections to enforcement, and his brutality earned trust and loyalty from his boss. This was at a time in the late nineties when French professional crime was changing from a family affair to an every-man-for-himself dogfight, and Coulfret was Dupris's pit bull, a sure bet in a shaky world.

More of Alex Coulfret's life comes into focus as I continue to read. The police reports include organizational charts, and Coulfret's name ascends the pyramid rapidly, almost month by month. Names and faces above his keep dropping off the chart, an indication a principal player died or went missing. It isn't difficult to hypothesize how. By the time I finish flipping through the files, Coulfret's name has replaced Dupris's at the top.

There are three pictures of Coulfret in the file. Two are from his previous arrests, when he was still a young man. He appears stocky, muscled, sinewy. He has a razor-thin mustache and an angular face, but his eyes crackle with intelligence. His expression—photographed while being arraigned—appears bemused, unperturbed, like the thought of going to jail is a minor inconvenience, a mosquito to be swatted. His nose is large and hooked and looks misplaced below those eyes.

The third picture is from a surveillance photo, taken just before his name appears on the list of deceased following the train derailment. The man has aged, and his mustache has grown into a full beard, but his expression is the same. He is standing in front of a restaurant, pointing to someone outside the frame. His physique remains athletic; he doesn't appear to have gone soft after he found himself at the top of the ladder. His nose is the same, a toucan's beak.

I snatch the photo from the file and hide it in my sock. The police won't have much use for it when they construct their new pyramid.

I'm able to glean a few more bits of information—he's never been married; he's childless; he speaks English, German, and Italian, as well as French.

I spot an interesting nugget in one officer's report. "**Plant listening device through Coulfret's nose? Avid wine collector. CI describes him as having an advanced sense of smell, proud of wine sniffing. Wire bottle with mic?**"

They must not have attempted this . . . at least I can't find a report or transcript centered upon a bugged wine bottle. Yet, it is nuggets like this that I file away. Hints to his personality. The man likes his grapes and fancies himself as a bit of a connoisseur. Perhaps I can build a strategy around this idea as I get closer to my quarry.

The rest of the reports offer nothing of consequence, and are perhaps most intriguing by what is absent from them. No one is sure where Alex Coulfret is currently living. Most of the reports don't buy his death, theorizing he moved to Switzerland or London or Rome. Others place him in a different section of Paris, the First or Second arrondissements, thinking maybe he changed his face, had some work done. Only a few think maybe the train crash death is real, that Occam's razor explains why their trail has gone dry, that the easiest explanation is usually the correct one. Coulfret died on that train and his body was cremated before proper identification could be done. End of story.

I'm looking for a different explanation. I don't believe a man like Coulfret ever leaves his neighborhood after exerting so much energy to rule it. It's a power source for him, a fuel, and moving away would wither that power as surely as starving a man would waste him down to skin and bones. The answer must be, as is so often the case, rooted in the past. The missing piece of information, the piece absent in the reams and reams of police records, the piece no officer cared to chronicle is this: what compelled Alex Coulfret to fake his death? And with so few people fooled, especially the police, it means he only needed someone to believe the ruse for a short time. So who is that someone, and was he fooled?

If I can discover the answer to that, then maybe I can discover where Alexander Coulfret is holed up now.

Officer Gerard is all smiles as I leave the police building.

"You will e-mail me when you get home, yes? Please call if you need anything or want some background information or need some spicy dialogue delivered the way a true French police officer talks, ha, ha. Maybe you'll have a part for this handsome face in your movie, yes? But I don't come cheap, ha, ha, ha, yes?"

I shake his hand, and he pumps it warmly, like he doesn't want to give it back, afraid his connection to Hollywood will evaporate like a mirage. I assure him I will shoot him an e-mail as soon as I return to my computer, and he finally nods and steps back into the station, mollified.

In my hotel room on the Rue de Balzac, I sit on the end of the bed and withdraw two photographs from my sock. One of Coulfret, the other of a low-level enforcer named Roger Mallery I managed to also nick right before I closed the file.

From what I am able to discern, Mallery is an up-and-comer within Coulfret's network, low-grade muscle who makes sure narcotics deals go down smoothly. He lives with his brother on Rue Stendhal in the Twentieth arrondissement in a one-bedroom flat and serves as a part-time butcher in a pork and chicken shop up the road. He has been picked up by French police for questioning on several occasions, most notably when three West African men tried to set up a rival supply chain in the Bastille district and ended up with their throats slashed by a serrated carver's knife. He didn't back down from the interrogation—"gave as good as he got," stated one detective's report—and was never arrested.

But one item stood out in their files, and I focused on it like it was written in red. Mallery has a side business with his brother, and he doesn't think the cops are aware of it. The French police are currently gathering information about this business, building a solid case to bring it down, aware that a bust here could serve as a key to opening a bigger box but so far they have yet to make a move on the two men.

So I'm going to move first.

When I walk into the butcher's shop, he is behind the counter, thinly slicing ham from a roasted pig.

"Hello."

"English?" he asks, just looking up for a moment before returning to his work.

"American."

"Pshhh. . . ." like the mere act of thinking about my country has given him a migraine.

In person, he is larger than I guessed from his picture, though he's not overweight. In fact, he seems skinny, fit, and yet somehow, well, *big*, like a blown-up photograph where the scale changes but the proportions remain the same. His face is dark and rough.

I wait for him to ask me what I want, but realize after a minute this is futile. He ignores me while continuing to slice razor-thin pieces of meat, his fingers working the blade hypnotically.

"Can I have a half-pound of bacon?"

Mallery looks up, grunts, and moves over to a small refrigerator from which he withdraws a paper package of meat. A minute later, and he's moving to the cash register.

"Eight-fifty."

I exchange euros for the package, and he considers me with sleepy eyes before returning to his cutting board.

When I don't leave the shop, he lifts his eyes again, waiting.

"I'm looking for a passport."

He stops cutting the pig and hammers the blade down in the butcher's board, then moves to a sink, washes and wipes his hands, drawing it all out in a puerile attempt at intimidation.

"You lose one?"

"No."

I keep my eyes level so he knows I mean business.

"What makes you tell me this?"

"I'm sorry. I might have been misinformed. Is your name Mallery?"

He just stares at me, non-committal.

"I was told you're the man to see about papers."

"Papers? What is this, papers?"

I nod like I've made a mistake. "I apologize. Thank you for the bacon."

I reach the door to the shop, and his voice stops me. "What kind of passport?"

I turn around, and though he's not grinning, his expression has shifted to agreeable.

"Italian."

"Five thousand euros."

"I paid three in Naples."

"Then go back to Naples."

I consider, then reach down to my wallet, but he clucks his tongue.

"Not here. The shop closes in two hours. Come back when you see me locking the door."

"I'll be here."

He resumes slicing the ham, the conversation over.

I follow Mallery through a maze of alleyways and side streets. His apron is off, hanging from a hook in the butcher's shop, I'm sure, but the smell of his work clings to him like a cloud: fresh-cut meat and viscera and blood. He's riding a ten-speed, and with his huge bulk, he looks ridiculous on top of the bicycle, like a clown riding a miniature.

When we reach a wide sidewalk, he slows to match my gait, side by side. Perched on the bike, he's at least a foot taller than me, maybe more.

"Who told you about me?"

I have anticipated this question. I know it'll be risky, but I don't believe he'll breach etiquette to check my story.

"Coulfret."

This doesn't elicit more from him than a raise of the eyebrows.

We stroll and roll along again in silence for a moment. I feel him wanting to say more, but he's fighting the urge. Finally, he loses the battle to stay cool. "You do work for him?"

"Yes."

"What kind of work?"

I point my finger like a gun and bend my thumb like a hammer cocking.

He raises his eyebrows again. "He didn't hire you to kill me, did he?"

I shake my head when I see he was trying to make a joke.

"How many jobs have you done for him?" he asks.

"You want to talk about this inside somewhere?"

He appraises me, then nods, appreciating my caution. We move along again in silence until the street takes a few more turns. Finally, we arrive at a courtyard. He dismounts, and swings the bike up on to his shoulder with no more strain than if he were lifting a sack of feathers. He presses a few buttons into a keypad, a security gate opens, and we move inside.

His apartment is more spacious than I would've thought: two bedrooms and a comfortable living room filled wall to wall with computer equipment. A log fire in the fireplace casts odd shadows over the room while it beats away the cold. A small kitchenette with a large refrigerator stands at the far end, behind a counter that separates the two rooms.

A man who can only be Mallery's brother looks up from a monitor as we enter. Roger swings the bicycle up on to a set of hooks attached to the ceiling and then gestures in the direction of his sibling.

"This is Luis."

"Hello."

The man nods, cautious.

"You mind if I pat you down?"

"Yes."

"You are carrying a weapon?"

"Several."

Mallery grimaces. He's not used to men like me, and it shows. I could've lied, could've told him I am unarmed and then wait to see how thoroughly he wanted to frisk me before I have to react, but he is testing me, testing to see if I'll let him be the alpha dog in his own home. My refusal lets him know what level of professional I am. He chews his lower lip, then foregoes the frisking.

He moves over to his brother, and they converse briefly in French.

Luis addresses me, his voice more resonant than his brother's, but deferential. "You need Italian passport, correct?"

"Yes."

"The Netherlands would be easier for you."

"I already have one for the Netherlands."

Luis smiles. "Okay . . . Italian it is. You have money, correct?"

"Five thousand euros. You'll get it after I've had a chance to inspect your work."

"Of course. You have a preference for a name?"

"Something common."

"Yes, okay. I will take a photograph first."

He directs me to a red line he has taped to the floor, facing his computer. After he clicks his mouse, he spins the monitor so I can take a look. I nod, and Mallery appears beside me, holding a bottle of wine.

"Let's move to the kitchen and have a drink while we wait."

He's had eight glasses and is laughing hard at my story, having lost track of my intake after I matched him the first three times he refreshed our drinks.

"So it comes down to this, I'm down to my last day to do this job, I've been fighting a goddamn fever for the better part of two weeks, I haven't really had time to formulate a secondary plan, so it's now or never and more and more it's looking like never."

"What time of year?"

"Middle of July and hot as hell. And you've never experienced heat until you've been in Houston in July. You can park your car right outside the door to your air-conditioned building, and by the time you take the ten steps and get behind the wheel, you're soaked through. Hundred percent humidity. Believe me, the last thing a gunman needs to battle is sweaty hands. Throw a fever on top of that and it's like I was walking around on fire."

Mallery laughs. "Please continue."

"So the mark is visiting this construction site across the street and the amount of time I have to pop him is predicated on an elevator ride—"

"Why did someone want your target dead, by the way?"

"I have no idea. I don't ask questions, I don't seek answers, I just kill the mark at the top of the page."

"Incredible."

"Yeah, so I know the bottom of that elevator disappears into a subterranean chamber, a bunker, and if he got down there, who knew when this bastard would ever emerge again, so if I was going to do it, I'd have to do it right then. I was completely out of time."

"Would I know this man?"

"You've seen his face in the business section of the *Wall Street Journal* if you follow stocks at all . . ."

Mallery waves like it's not important. He just wants me to keep going.

"So I'm in the high-rise across the street and he's in this elevator surrounded by muscle, and the wind kicks up, a scorching hot wind from the west, but I don't mind, the entire shot's maybe five hundred meters and I slow my breathing to a standstill and sight the target and this guy better have prayed his affairs are in order as the elevator car moves halfway down the building and I pull the trigger and . . . nothing."

"What?!"

"The gun jammed. Nothing and no time to check it and I am on my feet and scrambling down the five flights of stairs as fast as my legs can carry me."

Mallery is laughing so hard, tears have sprung to his eyes. He pours himself another glass.

"Down, down, two at a time and all I have on me is my Glock which is a damn fine gun but only at a range of thirty meters or less and I've never missed a target and I'll be damned if this asshole's gonna be my first."

"What did you do?"

"So I bust out of the door and look up and see that the target's elevator has about four floors to go and I am a city block away and since that building is under construction there is a barbed-wire fence surrounding it which is another good forty meters from the mark. I am taking all this in at once, and I'm not even thinking about traffic or pedestrians or civilians or police, I have to shut everything down and concentrate only on the moment, *this* moment, killing *this* target on *this* day, right then. It's hard to describe but the world becomes like a tunnel, everything else is blocked out, the only thing remaining in your vision is the strike point on your mark, where you have to shoot him to make sure he stays down forever.

"Even fighting this fever, I'm moving at a full sprint, plowing across the street and if a car slams on its brakes to keep from mowing me down, I don't hear it. An assassin isn't supposed to get his heart rate up, is trained to stay cool and collected, but my ticker is revving like a Lamborghini and my eyes are damned near blurry from the extra adrenaline accompanying my blinding headache and the gun in my hand feels like it's made out of cement."

"My God. . . ."

"The elevator car is almost to the ground, is just starting to slip below the surface and the mark and his half dozen bodyguards begin to disappear, first their feet, then their knees, and at that moment, all of them at once look at me, this wild man, red-faced, fisting a gun, sprinting across the street toward them like a guided missile and I can see their faces react, the two closest to their boss try to shove him down while stepping in front of him and then their torsos are disappearing and I have one shot, one chance in a million to thread the needle, an incredibly difficult shot even if all conditions are in my favor and I'm not half-dizzy with sickness. . . ."

"Yes? Yes?"

"And so I hit the ground, belly up, focus everything I have on my mark so that I can tell you how many freckles he has on his forehead, point the gun and pull the trigger just as the elevator dips below street level, gone."

Mallery is half-on, half-off his seat. His eyes are bulging, wide with anticipation, like a fish approaching a worm.

"What happened?"

"I missed."

"Ha ha ha ha! You missed? What do you mean, you missed?"

"I missed."

"Oh my God, you are too much. You and this story. This is the proverb, eh? The one who got away, ha ha ha ha?"

"I didn't say that."

Mallery looks back up at me, delighted there is a coda. "But you just said you missed!"

"I missed *then*. But he went home and I took some aspirin and killed him in his bed that night."

"Ha ha ha! Ha ha! Oh, you are destroying me here . . ."

Luis speaks up from the door, holding an Italian passport in his hand.

"Roberto Rossi."

"You should hear this story, Luis! This guy—"

Luis is smiling but his eyes are suspicious.

I stand up and take the passport from him, stumbling a bit so they'll think I'm inebriated. Roberto Rossi is the name Luis chose for me, a good one, as common in central Italy as John Smith. His work is professional, astute.

"You know what you're doing," I say to Luis. It never hurts to get a compliment in when someone is eyeing you warily.

"I've forged a few."

"I can tell."

Mallery stands, looking over my shoulder. "I may be the athletic one in the family, but Luis got all the brains. His work is perfect. That passport will not be questioned."

I pay Luis the five thousand euros and fend off Mallery's protests to stay for one glass more. Passport in hand, I leave the way I came.

Like I said, the key components in an ambush are information and timing. I've set the hook in Roger Mallery, and although I believe I could have persuaded him to talk about his principal employer Coulfret, Luis remains a wildcard, the smart brother, the one who does the work and keeps to the shadows.

Information and timing. And if I do my work properly, I'll continue to remove Mallery's defenses before he has a chance to engage them.

CHAPTER TWELVE

IF I WERE SVOBODA, AS SOON AS I RECEIVED WORD LLA-
NOS WENT DOWN WITH A KNIFE TO HER WINDPIPE IN
FRANCE, I'D HOP THE NEXT FLIGHT TO PARIS. I'd immediately head to a bank near the Charles de Gaulle airport where I keep
a safety deposit box loaded with weapons. Assassins store pistols, bullets, clips, knives all over the world, always near the airports. Airport
security being what it is has made traveling by air the most vulnerable time for a professional hit man, which is why I would get myself
armed as quickly as possible. And if I didn't personally have a stash of
weapons in Paris, I would arrange one through a capable fence.

Next, I'd use contacts in Paris, either with the morgue or the police or the underworld, to arrange a viewing of Llanos's body. I'd want fifteen minutes alone with the corpse. I'd examine the fatal wound and try to reconstruct in my mind the way it had gone down. Since I'm a Silver Bear, the "shelf above the shelf" as Archibald put it, I've been on the dispensing end of enough wounds to grasp a good idea of how this death unfolded.

If I were Svoboda, I'd now have a bit more knowledge about my mark, the man named Columbus I've been paid to kill. I'd know that for whatever reason, my target switched from his normal weapon of choice, a Glock handgun, to an inferior weapon, a stiletto blade. I'd know he used a neck shot, a straight puncture to the throat instead of a risky slashing motion. I'd know that he got the jump on the woman who was assigned to kill him. I'd know that he's better than I might have been told.

Then I'd look at Llanos's face—milky, empty—and I'd think about my quarry doing that to her, punching out her ticket when just the day before she had been young and lithe and alive. I'd think she was doing the same job I was hired to do, the same job I'm doing now, and my target discarded her like she was waste. I'd let my hatred build like a kindling fire, stoking it, fanning it, until it consumed every cell in my body.

And then, if I were Svoboda, I'd leave the stale trapped air of the morgue to walk back into the mottled throng of Paris. I'd close my eyes, breathing in the night, focusing my mind, feeding off my hate.

Then I'd open my eyes again, set my jaw, and begin to hunt.

Mallery is digging into a roasted duck at a sidewalk restaurant named the Café de la Comedie near the Louvre. The hand that holds his carving knife is blemished with the brick hue of bloody knuckles. Earlier, I watched him pound that hand into a gray-haired man's face in a warehouse next to a chocolate shop. I didn't quite catch why the gray-haired man deserved his beating, but as soon as he saw Mallery step through his door, the look of resignation on his face told me he knew it was coming. The old man took it pretty well, all in all.

I'm standing by the bar, drinking an Italian beer, watching him.

His phone buzzes, and he picks it up, reads something on the screen, then tries to work his thumbs over the little buttons, sending a text back. I wait, and eventually he gets up.

Sure enough, he spots me as he's heading to the bathroom.

"Roberto!"

I shoot him a cold look and he immediately clams up, his eyes as round as bicycle tires. "What?"

The best thing to do in this type of situation is to keep him off-balance, defensive.

"What were you doing with your phone?"

"Texting. . . ."

"Does Coulfret know you do that?"

He puzzles over that one. "I just text with my brother. I don't ever put anything on here that—"

"You ever see Coulfret use a mobile phone?"

"No, but—"

"That's because mobile phones lead to arrests."

"But I—"

"Never mind. I need your help."

It helps to shift directions like this, keep him back pedaling.

"What do you mean?"

"Come if you're going to come."

"What about my bicycle?"

"Leave it, goddammit."

And with that, I head out of the restaurant and into the street.

I can smell him before he reaches me. He must've slapped cash onto the table to cover his bill, made sure his bicycle was properly locked, and then hurried to catch up to me.

I don't look over my shoulder, don't acknowledge him, just keep walking forward. He whispers from behind me. "What are we doing?" Then catches up so we are walking side by side.

"A job."

He makes his fingers into a gun just like I did the day before, wiggles his thumb, and repeats, "A job?"

"Yes."

"Holy mother of Mary. What's the job?"

"To take down a target. Stay in the shadows."

He steps out of the sunlight closer to the wall, but can't manage to fit his whole body into the shade, as big as he is.

"Who is the target?"

"A woman. A hundred times out of a hundred I'd do this job alone, but Coulfret wants to see how you'll do."

Mallery swallows like he's trying to force down an egg. "Coulfret wants you to use me?"

"What'd I just say?"

"This woman. Who is she?"

"The wife of a man who shouldn't have tried to extort Alexander Coulfret."

"My God."

"Two of us working together is known in the game as a tandem sweep. That's what we'll be doing. . . ."

"I don't have a gun. I have a knife, and I have these. . . ." he says, rubbing the scabbed knuckles of his fist.

"You won't need either of them."

"But—"

"Just use your head and do exactly as I tell you, when I tell you, okay?"

"Yes, of course. What do you think? I do not listen? I will listen."

We round a corner, and fifty yards away stands a farmer's market selling fresh produce and meat and spices.

I hold up a Polaroid, a picture of a woman at a distance. "This is our target. She's in that market now. She won't leave it alive."

Mallery looks back and forth from the photograph to my face to the photograph, trying to commit it to memory like he's studying for exams but it's all happening too fast.

"Now here's your role in this . . . are you ready?"

Without hesitation, he nods.

"Shooting the target is easy, I could do it in my sleep, it's never a problem, listen!"

He's still riveted by the Polaroid in my hand and when I bark at him his eyes jump back to my face.

"The getting away is the problem, it's always the problem, it's the difference between more jobs or a life in prison or worse, so the escape has to be planned and precise and if you fuck this up in any way, I'll kill you myself."

He shakes his head; he won't fuck this up, he swears.

"Okay, good. Now you're the pigeon, the possum, the flop, okay? The misdirection, the diversion. You're where everyone casts his eyes so he doesn't see what's going on up the magician's sleeve.

"I want you to walk into that farmer's market and find the woman. When you see her, I want you to turn to the nearest produce stand and start in with a coughing fit. Can you cough?"

Immediately, he produces a cough so loud I think he's going to rattle a window.

"Not now, goddammit!" I say through gritted teeth and he stops like someone jerked a needle off a record. "Okay, while you're coughing, you won't hear anything except maybe the soft report of a silenced bullet, but out of the corner of your eye, you will see this woman drop. Do not look at her, don't you dare fucking look at her."

He shakes his head again; he won't look at her, don't worry about that.

"When you see the woman hit the ground . . ." I wait for a few pedestrians to pass, acting casual, and Mallery follows my lead. As soon as they're out of earshot . . . "When you see the woman hit the ground, I want you to stop coughing and walk away as calmly and as quickly as you can in that direction. Can you do that?"

He nods; he can do that.

"Now listen to me and listen to me like you've never listened to anything in your life. Do you know the story of Lot's wife? From the Bible?"

He shakes his head and I act like I'm even more frustrated with him.

"Well, you're going to want to look back, see if anyone's following you, see if a crowd has started to gather around the body, see if someone is fingering you or me or calling for the police, but you don't look back, don't do it, don't do it if the Madonna herself appears in front of you and screams at you to look back, do you understand me? You don't give any person at all a reason to remember your face. You just walk the fuck out of there, return to the café we just left, order yourself a glass of wine, and you fucking sit there until I come and get you, do you understand?"

"Yes. I walk away."

"You walk away."

"Yes."

"Good, now let's see what you're made of."

I clap him on the back and we set off for the market. He swallows hard, like he thought he'd have more time to prepare himself but here we are. It's sparsely crowded with local housewives picking up their daily bread and whatever vegetables and meat they plan to cook in the next couple of days. Few tourists are in this neighborhood this time of year, but the late sunset has brought in quite a few afternoon shoppers.

Our target is near a fruit stand, picking up and squeezing oranges. From where I hover over Mallery's shoulder, I can see him stutter-step as he recognizes her from the photo, a big clumsy signal a trained target would pick up on as easily as someone yanking an alarm. But we're in luck, the mark keeps picking up those oranges, in her own world when she should be paying attention to the wolf on her doorstep.

Mallery spins in place, wheels on a cheese seller's stand, and starts coughing like his lungs are exploding. It's a pretty damn good distraction, and most of the heads in the market spin in his direction, including the one belonging to our mark.

I come up beside her, my hand inside my coat pocket, and when she drops suddenly, Mallery does as instructed, he stops coughing and books it out of there, heading left out of the stand.

Usually, I would keep moving to put as much distance between the scene of the crime and myself before witnesses start tripping over themselves to see what happened. But I wait, following Mallery's ample gait with my eyes, watching to make sure he fights that urge and doesn't look back. Don't look back, don't look back, I'm willing him with my eyes and he doesn't turn, he does as he's instructed, and he rounds the corner at full stride.

When he disappears, I reach down and help the lady to her feet.

"You all right there, missy?"

"That's Ruby to you," she says with a smile.

When I reach the Café de la Comedie, Mallery is sweating. There is an empty glass in front of him, and I'm guessing he's drunk at least half of a bottle of wine. He almost upsets the table in his hurry to greet me, eager for my approval.

"It's done, correct?"

"Yes," I smile. "You did well."

"Just as instructed."

He's like a dog. Unsatisfied with just a pat to the head, he needs a scratch behind the ears.

"Yes."

"I did not look back."

"Good. Then no one will have followed you."

"I heard sirens. Sitting here. Waiting for you. I was worried."

I had seen police blowing past on the way to a motorcycle accident up the road. I didn't think about it at the time, but I'm glad Mallery believes the sirens belong to our affair.

"Never worry about me. Only yourself."

"We will do this again?"

I shrug. "We'll see what Coulfret says."

"You will tell him about today? How I composed myself?"

"Of course. Have another drink." I grab the waiter as he passes and order a fresh bottle of wine.

"I can't believe it," he says, true wonder in his eyes. "He usually uses me for. . . ." and he makes a couple of punching motions, a jab, an uppercut. Then pops one of his big fists into the other hand. "But this. . . ." He shakes his head. "How much, do you mind my asking?"

"How much what?"

"How much do you collect for a kill?"

I've got him now, though he doesn't know it.

"A hundred thousand Euros."

His eyes light up, filled with dollar signs. "Maybe I can . . . maybe he'll use me more for. . . ."

"Maybe. We'll see what Coulfret says."

A couple of glasses more and he's relaxed, giddy, speaking maniacally, the adrenaline getting the best of him.

It only takes a nudge from me. Information and timing.

"Let me ask you a question. I heard Coulfret faked his death a few years back."

"Oh, yes. Brilliant."

"Why would he need to do that?"

"You don't know this story? A story-teller like you?"

"Please."

"How much time do you have?"

"At least another bottle of wine's worth."

"Done!"

And he pounds the table as a third bottle arrives.

Alex Coulfret's first love wasn't a woman, but a building. He grew up in the Eleventh arrondissement, a block away from the Bastille, in a Haussmann-era residential edifice on the Rue Saint Maur. The building had twenty-two apartments, the smallest of which belonged to his father and mother. The apartment was in the basement, and they'd never have been able to afford if it hadn't been for his father's position as resident supervisor, a nice way the French have for saying "custodian."

The older of two brothers, Alex often accompanied his father on the daily tasks involved in keeping twenty-one tenants of a nineteenth-century building satisfied. Leaky pipes, peeling wallpaper, backed-up sewer lines, cracked windows, chipped floor tiles, faulty wiring, elevator repairs . . . Alex and his old man took care of all of them, working odd hours, always at the beck and call of the residents. In a building where everyone was of the same social stratum, the lower class consisted solely of this one family in this one apartment.

Alex spent his childhood learning every inch of that building. The crawl spaces, the roof, the rest of the basement with its clattering laundry machines, the copper pipes running behind the walls, the tiny balconies facing the courtyard, the floor drains leading down to the sewers. The residents looked on him and his brother with genuine affection, always ready with a pat to the head or an offered piece of peppermint candy. There were few children in the building, and the ones who were around Alex's age went to private schools and had their own sets of friends.

Alex's father died while carrying a bag of cement across the roof. His heart gave out: he dropped the bag, sat down, and died. Alex was fifteen, and it was like someone had cut out the best part of him. When the owner of the building, Mr. Hubbert, came round to pay his respects and tell his mother they would have two months to find a new apartment, Alex was ready. He showed the owner how to repair the washing machine, how to refill the split plaster on the second-floor corridor, how to keep birds from settling on the roof. He proposed that he would drop out of school and take over the duties of his father, that he knew the building better than anyone, that the free place to live for the three of them was all he needed . . . he'd find other ways to supplement his income. Mr. Hubbert was sympathetic and agreed to Alex's terms on a trial basis. If tenants complained, he would have to make changes. But no tenants complained.

A genial man on the second floor, a retired professor named

Mr. Condrey, gave Alex books to read to whittle away his evenings: Hugo and Dumas and Maupassant and Maugham. He taught him to dig deeper, behind the hero's journey and into the themes buried just below the surface: loss of innocence, jealousy, revenge as well as hope, patriotism, love. He found Alex to have a rapier mind and a thirst for intellectual stimulation. Alex, in turn, taught his brother, Jerome. If Alex couldn't go to school, he'd be damned if Jerome was going to miss a single day. Maybe he wasn't Jerome's father, but he damn sure acted like it.

The family still needed to put bread on the table, and Alex's mother took a job at a local bakery, selling croissants to tourists. Even bringing home the unsold pastries wasn't enough to keep the lights on, to keep wood in the fire. They needed more income, something, anything.

Alex had heard of Augustus Dupris from a pair of gossips who frequented the meat market. Dupris ruled the neighborhood (and several others), working and living out of a building two blocks away from Alex's. He had set up narcotics lines directly into Afghanistan and had profited greatly importing opium and heroin into the capital. In turn, he parlayed that business into providing protection, gambling, and prostitution in a city where most citizens turned a blind eye toward individual hedonism.

Still age fifteen, Alex presented himself to Dupris, explaining who his father had been, where he lived, what had happened to the family, what they were subsisting on, and how he could be of use to the professional criminal. He did his best to speak deferentially and intelligently, to make his case, explain how he could be an asset. He said he'd do any work the boss demanded.

Dupris slapped Alex across his face and told him to go back to school, go back to his family, to leave, and never to return. His men escorted him out of the building and Alex walked the two blocks home with his tail between his legs, but with a strong sense that he was being tested. Determination rose within him.

For weeks, Dupris couldn't leave the building without seeing Alexander Coulfret. The teen followed the middle-aged boss like a dog looking for scraps. When Dupris asked one of his men for a newspaper, Alex was already there, holding the latest edition. When he cut the tip off a cigar, he'd find Alex before him, holding out a struck match.

"You aren't going away?" the man finally asked the kid outside a hotel. "You aren't going to do as I tell you and leave?"

Alex shook his head.

Dupris smiled, like he couldn't quite figure out what made Alex's clock tick. "Then come to my building tomorrow at ten. And bring me some coffee."

Alex ran all the way home. That night, he cooked a ham for his mother and brother, the first meat they'd had in a week.

In the beginning, he delivered things for Dupris, sometimes to people who didn't want to be reached. He grew a reputation for being extremely clever, an intellectual cut above most of the mutts who worked for the boss. Where this might foster resentment, Alex had a way of recognizing trouble before it emerged, like a firefighter watering down fields to control the path of the flames. His cohorts couldn't help but like him, and he pulled their strings like a master.

He was a man who could talk at any level depending on to whom he was speaking, who knew the language, the idioms, the dialect of the streets, who could hold his own with the lowest pigeon on up to the boss himself. Guys he worked for found themselves working for him without quite understanding how the reversal had transpired.

By the time he was twenty, he had been arrested a couple of times but slipped any sentence harsher than a slap on the wrist. He taught Dupris how to maximize his gains by being merciless, by squeezing the suckers for every dime. In turn, his bank account grew.

His mother suspected something evil behind the income, but was so pleased to have food on the table, so pleased to see her younger son attending a private school for gifted students, that she instinctively knew better than to ask questions. She just wanted to put her feet up after a long day at the bakery and have wood to burn in the fireplace. Alex thought about telling her to quit her job—he was making more than enough to cover their expenses—but he resisted. The work kept her going, kept her vigorous, and somehow he knew it helped her to cope with the illicit money coming into the apartment.

When he turned twenty-three, he was Dupris's right-hand man, mostly working from the shadows. Dupris was starting to fear him as much as admire him, but the kid was like watching an avalanche cascade toward you and only being able to appreciate it. Alex was as devious as he was cunning, and he wasn't afraid to get his own hands dirty to prove a point.

All the while, he, his brother, and his mother stayed in that little apartment in the building on the Rue St. Maur. The residents still looked down their noses at the family in the supervisor's flat, and

Alex never strayed from fixing the faucets and the leaky pipes and the faulty heaters.

When Alex turned twenty-four, a real estate mogul named Saulter made a bid to buy the building. The original owner, Mr. Hubbert, was growing old and his only heir lived in the United States. The son wanted whatever price his father could get for the building. He had never set foot inside it and had no plans of moving back to Paris. Saulter made his offer. Paris was growing more expensive and the mogul felt if he could renovate the apartments, he could make a sizable profit. His plans for renovation also included getting rid of the current occupants.

Alex had by this time amassed enough wealth to buy the building himself for a fair price, and made an offer to Mr. Hubbert, but Saulter didn't give a damn about fairness. He was a capitalist in the true sense of the word; the biggest stack of dollars determined the winning bid, and he was prepared to outbid the son of the janitor.

Alex met with Mr. Hubbert for the second time in his life. The man was close to dying, was exhausted, and he spoke in a whining whisper.

"What do you want me to do, Alexander? What would you do? Ask yourself. I am doing this for my son in America. If you had come to me first, if there was no other choice, I would happily sell the building to you. I know you would take care of her like she was your mother or your wife. But Mr. Saulter came first and he will outbid you until you cannot match his offer. What would you have me do?"

Alex told him he was responsible for his own decisions.

"I know how you acquired your wealth," the old man said. "The things you've done for Augustus Dupris. If you say I *must* sell to you, then I will do so. I do not want trouble."

Alex repeated to the old man he was responsible for his own decisions, but assured him since he had shown Alex's family trust and kindness, no harm would befall him.

Mr. Hubbert told him he intended to sell the building to the mogul, Saulter.

Alex made two stops on his way home. First, he asked Dupris for an advance of two million francs so he might match Saulter's offer. But Dupris was drunk and with a woman and chose an inopportune moment to put Alex Coulfret in his place. He denied his request and called his prodigy a homesick fool. He offered Alex some wine and when he declined, protesting how important the building was to him, Dupris told him to lighten up and enjoy himself and to quit being so goddamned serious. Alex left enraged.

His next stop was Saulter's private residence in the heart of the Seventh arrondissement. When he went to bed that night, Saulter had three German shepherds and a German wife. When he awakened from a fitful sleep, he had none. Alex was waiting for him on a chair in the corner of the room. He told Saulter to move away from Paris and never look back, but not before Saulter phoned Mr. Hubbert to withdraw his offer for the building.

Augustus Dupris felt two emotions upon learning the next day that Alex Coulfret was the new owner of the building he had grow up in on the Rue de Maur. Anger and fear. He did not like the way those two emotions made him feel, like a weight had settled in his stomach. He did not like the way his second-in-command had circumvented his decision-making. He did not like the way his other foot soldiers looked at Coulfret—the same way they used to look at him.

He decided to hire some dark men. He might have been successful except that a low-level hood named Martin Feller saw the future and made the decision of his life, rolling the dice and putting his hat in the ring with Alex. He had overheard Dupris bragging about the contract he had taken out on his right-hand man's life. And so Feller tipped off Coulfret.

Alex could've brought it to a head the moment he found out about the hit, could've walked the two blocks to Dupris's house, forced his way in, and shot the man and everyone who stood with him. God knows he wanted to. But the chess player inside him won out; instinctively, he knew that if the last rung of the ladder on the rise to the top is stepped on with brute power instead of *earned* through cunning, through artful intelligence, then his reign would always be contested, would always be marked with bloodshed.

So he faked his death. He waited for the right opportunity, then put money in the palms of a trusted few, and convinced Dupris and his hired killer that they had lucked out, that nature and a fickle god and two vehicles colliding had done their dirty work for them, that sometimes things have a way of working themselves out.

A week went by, two. Dupris inquired about buying the building himself, but Jerome Coulfret, the brother, resisted. His education had instilled in him a keen business sense, a sense that would serve him well in the jewelry trade years later. The ownership of the building suddenly became important to Dupris, like having a tangible trophy to put in his case, a symbol for the rest of his men to see what happened if they chose to tangle with the boss. He became obsessed with owning it, refusing to let Alex's pissant brother keep this prize from him.

Recognizing the volatility of the situation, Jerome told Augustus Dupris he feared for his and his mother's safety, and he wanted assurances that if Dupris bought the building, no harm would befall them. Dupris agreed but Jerome wanted a commitment in person; he insisted that Dupris come to his small janitor's apartment in the basement of the building and he would sign over the papers in front of witnesses.

Dupris brought three of his most trusted bodyguards, men whom he used for intimidation and enforcement. They entered the building on the Rue de Maur, suspecting nothing. They paraded down the hallway, suspecting nothing. They piled into the cramped elevator and pressed the appropriate button, suspecting nothing.

The cable snapped and the elevator car plummeted, dropping thirty feet in three seconds and slamming like a thunderclap into the concrete foundation. It bounced, crumpling like a crushed soda can, and came to rest at an eighty-degree angle at the bottom of the shaft, like a domino about to topple. Dupris and his men were injured, sure, but nothing life-threatening. That part would come in a moment. They were more shocked and confused, still trying to figure out what happened.

The doors just above their heads pried open from the outside, and light spilled into the car. They looked up expectantly, eager for aid, for someone to help them out of the collapsed car.

A ghost stared down at them: Alexander Coulfret, back from the grave, resurrected in a building he knew better than anyone. His face was sinister; there was triumph in his eyes. He glared at the men, as helpless as sardines packed in a tin, and started firing.

Maybe Mallery didn't tell the story quite so fully, but he laid out the broad strokes, and it didn't take much digging to fill in the details. I've found that once you possess a few nuggets, it's much easier to pry the whole story out of people. If you listen, a neighborhood will talk.

CHAPTER THIRTEEN

HE'S IN THE BUILDING ON THE RUE DE MAUR, OF THAT I'M CERTAIN. And either he's a complete recluse, holed up in a tiny apartment, running his kingdom from the shadows, or he had his face changed, happy with the way the police or perhaps his rivals were fooled by his accidental death ruse. My guess is the latter. The men in his organization are way too deferential for Coulfret to be a shut-in. That kind of power comes only from a firsthand, iron-fisted rule. The fact that the police never quite bought the ruse tells me he didn't need to use it for long.

To get to him, to end this, I have two choices. Try to infiltrate his building, or try to flush him toward a place of my choosing.

I mentioned a few ways I go about gathering information: I can steal it. Or I can force someone to give it to me under duress. Or, like with Mallery, I can feign friendship in order to extract what I need. But there is another way, one I've employed on occasion. It's tricky, but it can be effective.

I buy a cheap camera from a souvenir shop near the Rue St. Denis and start scouring the sidewalk for prostitutes. The ladies populate this street at all hours of the day, dressed in their dystopian view of evening wear, ready to approach a john for business as soon as his gaze lingers for more than a fleeting moment. There is no cream of the crop here, no high-priced whores, no beautiful young women lost under a layer of makeup. The women on the Rue St. Denis are well past the age and weight when they should be parading their wares.

My eyes settle on a particularly homely sample and I speak to her as best I can in French.

"How much?"

"Thirty."

"How would you like to make three hundred?"

Her eyes reflect the age-old battle between fear and avarice. I can read her thoughts as easy as if she spoke them aloud: *Whatever he wants me to do can't be good for my health, but three hundred euros is more than I've made in a month.*

"What for?"

"To ride in a taxi and take some photos."

"With you?"

"By yourself."

"Psssh." She waves at me like I'm insane.

"I have a taxi waiting."

"I don't know what cheat this is. . . ."

"No cheat. Here's thirty just for listening to me. Here's two hundred and seventy, which I'll give you if you take this camera in that taxi and fill the camera with photos of the second block of the Rue de Maur. You'll be back here in thirty minutes."

Her brain is trying to calculate the percentages of risk versus reward but the entire effort is simply too much and her eyes refocus on the money in her hand and the rest of it within grabbing distance.

"You do this right and there'll be more jobs like it, all over town, paying even more."

"Just take photos?"

"When you approach the block, hold the camera like this, here, not up to your eye, but down at the bottom of the taxi's window. Click, wind here, click, wind . . . do it on both sides of the street. I've instructed the taxi to drive slowly, but not too slowly. Take as many as the camera will allow. The taxi will then return you here."

"Fifty more now," she croaks. Two of her teeth are missing and the remaining ones are stained with lipstick.

"Not a euro more until I have a full camera."

She grimaces and then shrugs, takes the camera, and waddles over to the taxi.

I keep my word when she returns. She'll try to remember me, the man wearing a hat and dark glasses, should I come back to the Rue St. Denis, but by that evening, I have no doubt alcohol will have wiped her memory clean. Besides, I have no plans to return to that particular street.

I develop the pictures at a one-hour photo on the opposite side of town, far away from the Bastille district Alexander Coulfret calls home. Nothing from the photo-shop worker indicates that he gave my pictures anything more than a cursory look. And why would he have noticed anything more than typical tourist photos of a sleepy Parisian block?

Back in my hotel room, the photographs are laid out across an ottoman I'm using for a desk. The whore wasn't exactly Ansel Adams, but she did an adequate job, all things considered. She took thirty-six photos, covering the entire block, and only had her thumb in one frame.

Here's what I learned that I didn't already know by way of the internet. The block has five buildings on either side, with a series of shops fronting most of them. The adjacent buildings to the one owned by Coulfret contain apartments above a pastry shop and a dressmaker's boutique. The location where a shop would be at the bottom of Coulfret's particular building is a mystery; paper blinds fill the windows.

Across the street stands a trio of similar buildings, containing two clothing stores and a pharmacy. All six shops—including the empty one—have cameras facing the street, sophisticated equipment for disparate places, all made by the same manufacturer. It seems Coulfret's real estate ambitions have grown to include most of his block. I wonder if all six buildings are connected, and, if so, how. Paris has an extensive underground sewer system, and perhaps he's taken advantage of it.

The whore's photographs also reveal men sitting with a certain lassitude on three benches positioned on both sides and across the street from Coulfret's front door. Six hard-looking men, three benches. My guess is they rotate out regularly, and who knows how many more are waiting inside that shop with the papered-over windows?

Storming the building is starting to look like an ugly proposition, a long-odds loser.

Ruby Grant smiles over her cup of coffee. We're on the Left Bank, in the back of a café once frequented by Hemingway and Fitzgerald and Joyce.

"I'm worried about you, Columbus. For a loner, you're starting to ask me to hook up with you quite a bit."

"Who says I'm a loner?"

"Every file ever written about you."

"What do the files say about you?"

"If I see any, I'll let you know."

"You're a blank slate. . . ."

"With this face, I'm sure a few people have noticed me. Right before I shot 'em."

"You ever think about checking out?"

She looks at me sideways. "Of the game? Nah, I'd just waste away. You?"

"Just thoughts."

Goddamn, I have no idea why I'm telling her this. It's like I'm floating a balloon. Maybe if I can practice here with Ruby Grant, I can persuade myself to put this life behind me the next time I see Risina. Jesus, is that it?

I discover a tiny bit of disappointment in Ruby's eyes.

"Well, I'd stop thinking those thoughts if it were me. You start going down that road, you don't realize you can't turn around until you hit a dead end."

I nod. "Ahhh, I'm just blowing air. This life is all I got."

She knows I'm snowing her now, but she's happy to get off the subject.

"Archie really has a file on me?"

"He's got a file on everyone he ever met. Says you shot a cigarette out of his mouth once in Boston."

"Well, that's true."

She laughs, an effortless, warm sound.

"All right . . . you know so much about me, time for you to 'fess up."

She spreads her hands out like she's ready for me to ask anything.

"Tell me how you started pulling trigger for your brother. I've never seen that before, a brother–sister, fence and assassin."

"Ahh, it's nothing. I worked for him for a while . . . helped him put files together . . . got into places he probably wouldn't be able to get into. A couple of years at that, and I told him I was itchy to try it."

"And he just said 'okay'?"

She looks at me out of the tops of her eyes. "Oh, I get it. I see what you're doing here. You wanna hear about my first time?"

It's my turn to shrug.

"Fine, fine. You can be the first to hear it, then, other than Archie who knew the story anyway. Just go get me one of them macaroons they got up in the window there and then settle back, 'cause I got a tale to tell."

I do. And she does.

"The first time—you never forget the first time, you know what I'm saying? Well, Archie was worried about me, even though I was born for this, truth be told. So he just kept putting it off and putting it off until I told him, 'Archie, if you don't hurry up and give me an assignment, I'm liable to just go ahead and make you my first target.' At this point, I'd been following marks for at least a couple of years, and Archie knew I could handle my business, but he was reluctant to let me out of the starting gates.

"Finally, he relents, looks at me sideways, and hands me this file."

"A creampuff," I offer.

Ruby laughs. "Oh, yeah. A cakewalk. An easy-greasy, 'stroll down Broadway and collect two hundred dollars as you pass Go' kind of hit. Archie'd just been waiting for a tasty peach like this so I could pop my soda."

"I don't blame him."

"Shit, I don't either. I didn't. Not then, at least. So I look over the file, and it's exactly what you'd expect. Some mid-level guy works in a paper mill, up for a union position and I guess someone didn't think too favorably of that. This guy, shit, I don't even remember his name, Black or Brown or something like that, we'll just call him Brown, well, Brown's got a routine he's been following every work day for twenty years. Gets up—"

"Family guy?"

"No, never been married, lives alone, all by his lonesome. . . ."

It's my turn to laugh, "Jesus."

"I know! Anyway, gets up, goes to this little diner slash coffee shop, eats two eggs, two pieces of toast, two strips of bacon . . ."

"Two cups of coffee."

"You got it. Then he drives in to work, punches the clock, works his eight, punches out, hits a bar named George's along with half his co-workers, and heads home. Wash, rinse, repeat."

"A creampuff."

"Ain't that the truth. A guy stuck in a rut. A thousand ways to drop this guy and all of 'em as clean as a whistle, as my mom would say."

She stops to take a bite of the macaroon, then swallows quickly so she doesn't lose momentum.

"So here's the kicker. Archie tag-teams it—"

"Shit."

"Yeah. Wants me to double up with a long-time shooter he's got in the stable, name of Tuesday—Tuesday Schmidt or something like that. Ever heard of him?"

I shake my head, and she waves like it doesn't matter.

"Why would ya? Anyway, this guy's pulled jobs for Archie for as long as I've known him and I've read his file and he only works once in a blue moon, but he seems good to go, so whatever. I mean, I'm annoyed, but whatever.

"Archie assures me this bagman is going to just show me the ropes, but I'll get the kill shot, and I guess that's what matters, because the truth of it is . . . how will I react? It's one thing to follow a mark and make notes in a file, another to actually—ah, hell, you know what I'm talking about. Jesus, how long is this story? You sick of it yet?"

"No, believe me, I'm entertained."

"I'll try to pick up the pace just the same. So Archie puts us together and I meet Tuesday for the first time, and he's not at all what I was expecting. Maybe his file needed updating or something, but this guy is a biscuit away from three hundred fifty pounds and he's gotta be at least sixty years old."

"Christ."

"Tell me about it. I start thinking maybe Archie's doing the favor for *this* guy, not me. So we ride around together and we stake Brown for at least a week to make sure the file's up to snuff, though I know it's going to be. Say what you want about my brother, but Archie can put a file together, that's for sure.

"Anyway, we sneak into this mark's house when he's at work to get the lay of the land, we eat breakfast at the diner, we even get into his mill and scout it out, all the homework, you know. Tuesday's pretty entertaining, actually, got a million stories he's spooling out like fairy tales—the moral of this story is 'don't leave your safety on,' the moral of this story is 'carry an extra clip in your bag'—that type of thing. He's got me in stitches half the time we're working this job.

"Finally, seven days of sitting in the car with him and he leans over and asks, 'how you wanna handle this?' I don't even think two seconds and I say, 'hit him when he gets home after the bar.' The fat man shrugs and says suits him fine, see ya tomorrow night, and that's that.

"Of course, I don't sleep that night, I don't eat the next day, I'm all geeked up like it's Christmas morning, you know. Now I got to wait around all day since I'm the one who said let's hit him at night, so I end up getting in my car and following the mark to make sure he's still sticking to his pattern—"

"Don't tell me you jumped the gun."

"No, not at all. I just wanted to watch this guy and see what's what. And let me tell you, it was a hell of a feeling, knowing he was gonna die and him not knowing it . . . does that make sense?"

"More than you know."

"I got a confession to make. I like the way it felt."

"Yeah. It's the nature of the beast."

"You got that right. Anyway, I make sure the target goes to the bar after work like normal, and then I head over to meet Tuesday at the meeting point where we decided to hook up. He's there when I get there, and I climb in his sedan, take a look at him, and let me tell you, he's not looking so hot. His face is red and he's sort of sweating all over.

"'What's up?' I say, and he just shrugs and says, 'nothing.'

"'You all right?' I say, and he mutters something like 'why wouldn't I be?' and we take off for Brown's pad.

"I'm thinking, 'oh man, tell me this old veteran don't have cold feet or isn't shaky or something . . .' not on my first pull, you know? 'Please tell me Archie didn't tag-team me with a guy who's suddenly having second thoughts about the shooting game.'

"So I got one eye on Tuesday and one eye on the prize and we wait and wait and eventually Sweet Georgia Brown comes home and I'm out the car door three seconds after he heads inside.

"Tuesday climbs out of the front seat and blocks my way and I'm like, 'listen, old buck, if you lost your nerve . . .' and he stares bullets at me and sort of growls like a junkyard dog and says, 'wait, goddammit. You gotta let the mark settle in and catch him with his head on the pillow. Patience, lady, patience.'"

"I give him my best stink eye but he's having none of it, and he's right after all, but I swear something's off about him. His face is splotchy, bright red in the cheeks, white on the forehead, and he's dripping sweat, and I don't know what to think.

"So we wait and wait and wait some more, and I'm listening to Tuesday's heavy breathing like he's on some phone sex line for what seems like a week, and finally the clock hits the hour and I nod at him and he shrugs and opens his door.

"We check the street and there ain't a soul in sight at two in the morning, so we head up to the house. I pull out a pick but check this out, the motherfucking mark doesn't even lock his front door."

I chuckle and she leans forward, eyes dancing.

"Tell me about it. This ain't just a cakewalk, it's a trip around the whole goddamn dessert bar. So we move into the living room and I can hear Brown snoring in the back so I make a hand signal like I'm gonna go take care of business, and I look over at Tuesday and the man's face is stark white, all color gone, like I'm looking at Casper the fat fucking ghost. He's holding his arm like this and I swear I have no idea what the hell's happening and right then he topples over, all three hundred fifty pounds of him falls sideways like a build-ing coming down, right on a glass coffee table, I shit you not."

"Heart attack?" I‚can't keep the chuckle out of my voice.

"You got it. And this coffee table doesn't just break, it explodes. I mean it sounds like someone set a bomb off in the room. KA-BOOOM!"

She smacks the table for emphasis.

"Before I know what's happening, I mean I'm just processing this shit, I turn my head to see Brown, buck naked, standing in the doorway to his bedroom, holding a sawed-off shotgun.

"My heart's beating like a drum and I remember the thought going through my head . . . I'm wondering what we must look like, a dead fat guy collapsed on his coffee table and me looking like I do, holding a gun in my hand.

"I don't know if he thinks we're burglars or what, but I guess he figures it out pretty damn fast, because he points both barrels at me and pulls the trigger."

I raise my eyebrows and Ruby grins, anticipating my surprise.

"Click. That's all he gets. You think I didn't notice that gun under his bed when I staked his house? I know I'm not supposed to touch anything but I wasn't going to take any chances. So I took the shells out of the barrels and left it right where it was.

"Good thing."

"Damn straight."

"And Brown?"

"I knocked the surprise right off his face."

"And Tuesday?"

"Never saw Wednesday again."

I give her the slow clap and she pantomimes a curtsy as we both laugh.

"I'm impressed. You tell a good story."

"Now you know more about me than anyone in the game."

"I know I better check to make sure my gun's loaded if you're coming for me."

"You're right about that." She stands. "I'll be right back," and with that, she heads to the sign marked "WC."

Like her brother, Ruby Grant has grown on me quickly. We are opposites—we approach this job from radically different directions—and yet maybe that's not such a bad thing. Maybe I can learn from her as much as she learns from me. Like getting inside a mark's head, maybe getting inside Ruby's head will show me a different angle, a different way to navigate this business.

She drops two fresh macaroons on the table as she takes her seat. "Pistachio and vanilla," she says. "You gotta try both."

"No, thanks."

"More for me," she shrugs as she bites into the green one.

Swallowing, she starts in with "All right, then. Enough about my humble beginnings. Let's focus on the matter at hand. What's going on and where do I fit in?"

"I'm going to take out the man who put the hit on me."

"He dies, no one to pay out the contract, the hit goes away?"

"That's the idea."

"So where is he?"

"Holed up in one of six buildings on the Rue de Maur. Heavily defended. He's known the neighborhood and the buildings his entire life. Oh, and I don't know what he looks like . . . I'm pretty sure he had his face changed."

She waits, her expression unreadable. Then she manages, "Shiiiit." Just like her brother.

"I know."

"What d'you need me for? Sounds like the same type of cream-puff as my Mr. Brown."

"Uh-huh."

"You got blueprints of the six buildings?"

I shake my head.

"Any of 'em?"

I shake it again.

"You know how many guys he's got?"

I just keep shaking.

"Fuck you, Columbus. I mean seriously, fuck you."

"I'm not going to go *in* there. . . ."

"No shit you're not."

"I'm going to bring him out to me."

She nods now, regaining interest. "Okay, okay. Now we're talking. How do you plan to draw him out?"

She leans back and waits for me to paint the picture. I give her the basics while she finishes her macaroons. The table we occupy in the back corner has allowed us both to speak freely, as opposed to the States where we might have had to worry about hovering waiters. Here, the staff usually gives you all the room you need.

After I finish, she leans forward. "Okay. Okay. I dig where this is going."

"Good. You're in, then?"

"Depends."

"On?"

"I talked to Archie today. He wants to be your fence when this is over. That's why I've been hanging around. I'm supposed to seal the deal."

Well, there it is. I knew it was coming; I just didn't know when.

"I'm not sure there's going to be much more for me when this is over."

"Uh-huh."

"I've put in quite a few years now, and I'm still young. I lied when I said it was just a thought. I've been thinking about it more in the last month than in the previous thirteen years. There might be a way out for me."

"How long you been giving yourself that speech?"

"Not too long."

"No, I didn't think so." She shifts so she can look me straight in the eyes. "Listen, if you think there's an escape hatch for you, I'll tell Archie not to stand in your way."

I nod, and she leans forward again. "But if you can't get out—if you try it and things go sour—then he's gonna want you in the fold."

I sit back and rub my hands on the top of my head and think of Risina and then of a dropped silver handle on a stopped silver wagon and think of giving everything to her by giving everything away. And then my eyes fall on Ruby sitting in front of me, in this world, my world, and something in me keeps seeking her out, again, a few times during this hunt, a game in which I'm more hunted than hunter, and my instincts are out in front of my intellect. Do I want Archibald Grant to be my fence? Have I been angling for that without even realizing it? And what does that say about my plans to give this life up? Maybe I'm deceiving myself.

"Okay."

She doesn't ask for confirmation, doesn't want to prolong my internal conflict. She's the kind of woman who knows what an "okay" means without having to dig it out and analyze it.

We settle the bill, head to the front of the café to make plans for our next rendezvous and maybe we're being cavalier and maybe we're too comfortable and maybe there were signs, the way there were signs in that coffee shop on the day all this began.

I look up to see Roger Mallery riding down the street atop that goddamn bicycle and his eyes find us, and the look of confusion on his face lasts for what seems an eternity as his mind works out the mechanics . . . that I told him I was working for his boss Coulfret, that I needed his help on an assassination, that our mark was the very much alive girl standing next to me, that the whole thing was a lie . . . I can see it all come together for him, one plus one can only equal fucking two, and he must spot my eyes narrowing, hardening, because he swallows, lowers his chin, and starts pumping his pedals desperately, like a sprinter. His bike responds by hurtling down the street as though it has been fired out of a cannon.

Ruby recognizes Mallery just moments behind me and I think she says something to me, but my legs are already moving, and I dart across the street and barrel as fast as I can down the sidewalk.

As large as Mallery is, he sure knows how to work that fucking bike, and his lead grows as he cranes his neck practically under his right armpit to make sure I'm not gaining on him.

Three workers are unloading boxes out of a black delivery truck with the engine idling, and if luck wants to spin around on a dime then I'm sure as hell going to take advantage of it. I'm in the driver's seat and throwing the truck into gear and ignoring the shouts of the angry workers and if there are any police loitering around for the next couple of blocks then I'm just going to have to deal with them later because I cannot let this man warn Coulfret.

He looks back for me on the sidewalk and then spots me behind the wheel of the truck and I discover a moment of panic in his eyes. Often, panic in your enemy can provoke a mistake, a stutter, an opening to his defeat. But it can also lead to a surge of adrenaline, a dip into the reservoir of energy he has buried inside him.

Mallery turns back, grits his teeth, and recognizes an advantage. There is traffic in the one-way street up ahead, and he doesn't have to stop. He zips up a lane of his own creation, between idling cars and the rigid curb. I slam on my brakes and just catch a blur as a Vespa whips past me, Ruby atop it hunched over the handlebars like a jockey on a thoroughbred, and then she rounds the corner moments behind Mallery. At least one of us chose the right vehicle.

Fuck this. I hop the delivery truck over the curb and ride up the sidewalk, scattering pedestrians, bouncing on faulty hydraulics like I'm inside a washing machine. I spin the wheel and the truck responds, swinging to the right, somehow keeping on all four tires, and my fears are realized, no sign of Mallery on his bicycle or Ruby on the Vespa and a cluster of additional traffic ahead. I roll up a block, my head on a swivel, eyes scanning everywhere, and I catch just a glimpse of an overturned moped lying like a felled beast in the middle of the street of the adjacent block.

I jump out of the truck without bothering to throw it into park, ignore the foot traffic on the sidewalk, and as I get closer, I can see Mallery's bicycle also lying flat on its side, looking alien in that way bicycles do when they're not upright, half on and half off the curb, front tire spinning.

Again, I'm stymied, no sign of the big man or Ruby Grant, and then I hear the distinctive crack of a pistol firing. It came from somewhere up and to my left, and I duck my head and sprint inside the residential building in front of me. Something is troubling about that crack; Ruby prefers a high-caliber weapon, a .44, and the crack sounded sharp, quick, more like the pop of a kernel of corn, and I'm not sure about any of it, what exactly I heard, what was an echo, what was amplified, but that damn butcher better not have a gun. I've been with him twice before and never known him to carry a firearm.

I fly up a flight of stairs, mounting them two at a time, and almost shoot Ruby in the head. She's crouched against a wall, looking amused, like she is expecting me, and what took me so goddamn long, and isn't this whole affair a lot of goddamn fun. I don't know how she does it—I'd like to think it's all a façade—but I've been around her enough now to think maybe she's found some way to swallow the strains of our chosen profession and fuel it into something else. What? Passion? Maybe she's wired differently. Maybe she just enjoys it. Maybe I'm more like Ruby than I'd care to admit.

She smiles as I lower my gun and ease my index finger off the trigger.

"He's carrying a pea-shooter. Got a shot off at me and ducked around the corner."

I look above her head. A fresh bullet hole is plugged into the wall.

"He have a way out?"

"I don't think so. Just got a quick scan of the building when I headed inside, but I think those stairs behind you are the only way down."

She taps a ceramic "Fire Emergency Exit Plan" sign next to her head. The writing's in French but the map is clear: it displays the floor plan with a broken line showing a route to the stairs behind us in case the building goes up in flames.

I see something else on the map and point to it. "It's not the only way up."

Her face falls, now inspecting the sign while wrinkling her nose. "How much time you think we have?"

She's talking about police response time—someone reported the delivery van stolen, someone witnessed the chase, someone spotted the overturned Vespa and bicycle, someone heard the gunshot.

Still, it's a lot to add up for even the most opportune French police officer. So before enforcement becomes a nuisance, I'd give us. . . .

"Fifteen minutes. Maybe more if we're lucky."

"Dammit." She pushes away from the wall and we stalk toward the corner, instinctively deciding that I go high and Ruby take low. We swing around the bend in perfect synchronicity, prepared to duck and fire at the same time, but Mallery isn't waiting for us.

I kick open the door to the roof, catch just a glimpse of the sun reflecting off of metal, and pull Ruby back as a tempest of bullets pounds into the open door frame. A second late, and we would've both caught taps to the head.

"Well, that was your one chance," I call out.

"Go to hell, you lying son of a whore."

I can see him through a wedge in the doorway. He has his gun hand up but keeps throwing glances over his shoulder, at the roof's ledge.

"Don't do it, Mallery. You're too big of an oaf to think you can jump across that alley."

His face loses color as he realizes I can see him, and he sprays the doorway with another volley of bullets.

"Can he make it?" Ruby whispers.

I shrug and then peer through the slit where the door is hinged to the wall, where I can see it on his face. I was hoping for resignation but instead he has resolve, and he's measuring out the steps it'll take him for an adequate runway before he launches.

Ten steps. It's not going to be enough. He's just too big and I doubt he has much experience in long-jumping and he keeps the gun pointed at the doorway, but he's going to have to lower it and turn his back on me to make the leap. He breathes once, twice, filling his lungs with oxygen, psyching himself up. Now or never.

I shoot him square in the back, toppling him before he takes his fourth step. He spills forward, headfirst like he's trying to dive into a swimming pool, five feet short of the ledge.

Ruby and I approach cautiously, but I know from the way he

dropped, the bullet took his life immediately. The leak on this faucet is plugged. Or so I think.

"Let's skedaddle," Ruby says, but there are two objects out in front of Mallery's body. He must've been clutching both of them when he fell. One I knew would be there: his weapon, a little Browning automatic.

The other is his phone.

I stoop, pick it up, and look at the face. It only takes a moment to realize what Mallery had time to do while he held us off at the stairwell door.

"What is it?"

"He texted his brother."

The text reads: ROBERTO ROSSI'S A FRAUD. TELL COULFRET.

I look down at Mallery's body. Somehow, his chin is up and his corpse is looking at me. I'm not certain, but I think he is smiling.

An ambush is information and timing, but a footrace boils down to improvisation and speed. I have Mallery's phone in my hand and there has been no return text, so I'm hoping his brother Luis hasn't yet received the message. Surely he would've tried to call or text back. Maybe I'm lucky and he doesn't have his phone with him.

Ruby and I scamper out of the building without hearing any sirens and finally something is going right for us and maybe good luck can build up like bad luck or at least keep the hounds at bay.

We arrive at an empty cab stand with two idling taxis and time moves no slower than when you're reliant on someone else to drive you somewhere.

"Nothing on the phone?"

"Not yet."

"Then we jump this bastard before he gets the message. Easy as pie."

"I haven't had a good pie in a long time."

"Well, don't look at me," Ruby says. "I wouldn't know where to begin to bake a motherfucker. But I'm sure it's easy."

"Maybe yes, maybe no."

"Look, even if this boy gets the text . . . he calls your mark and. . . ."

"He can't call. Coulfret doesn't use phones. Mallery told me that when I first saw him texting his brother."

"Even better. But let's say he gets to your mark, and warns him you're on to him, that doesn't give the big boss a whole hell of a lot more than he already had."

"He'll have my face."

"What?"

"Passport photo. The brother is a forger . . . phony passports."

"That was your in?"

"That was my in."

"Goddamn."

The cab pulls over near the Bastille and I throw a wad of euros over the seat and we're out the door. The plan, if you can call it that, is to move backwards from the Rue de Maur to Mallery's apartment. If Luis is coming to warn Coulfret, maybe we can intercept him along the way.

It's a ten-minute walk, even at a hurried pace, but there's no sign of him and the phone in my hand remains silent. I plug in the code to the security gate I saw over Roger Mallery's shoulder the first time I came here, and Ruby and I step into the courtyard. Luis has two ways to exit his building, twin stairwells at either end of the entrance. I choose east and Ruby takes west, and we enter the stairwells simultaneously.

The corridor is darker than I remember, but that may be a mind's trick; I was in control the last time I was here, and I am on the defensive now . . . ever since Roger Mallery rode by at the most inopportune time in this city of millions and sometimes coincidence is just coincidence but it's unlikely, I realize now in this lightless stairwell, damn unlikely. Occam's razor would be slicing the shit out of this one—the most reasonable explanation is that Mallery was tailing me, and I don't know where my head was but I didn't spot him and that may be the most worrying development of this entire fucking affair.

I turn up the second flight of stairs when the hallway lights up in a bluish glow and my hand vibrates, indicating an incoming text on Mallery's phone.

Three words: GOING FOR HELP. And right then I hear a gunshot, definitely Ruby's gun, and a scream of pain, definitely Ruby's scream.

"Oh, Jesus," I think and maybe say aloud, but I'm already breaking out of the stairwell and sprinting the length of the hall, passing dozens of apartment doors, one of which is opening to investigate the commotion but I cannot hesitate, just plow through the west stairwell door and Ruby is on her back on the landing with a butcher's knife buried in her arm, just below the shoulder.

She's not shrieking, just angry, steeling herself to yank out the knife.

"No!"

"What the fuck do you mean, 'no!?'"

Well, if she's healthy enough to snap back at me, then she's going to be okay.

I pull my shirt off. "Use this to stanch the bleeding," and before she can bark at me again, I toss her my hotel key . . . "Room 202. Bag under the bed."

I'm already flying down the stairs when she yells, "Drop his ass, Columbus!" after me.

A footrace may be improvisation and speed, but now it's just speed and he's got a block and a half on me as I blast out of the building and sprint after him.

Unfortunately for Luis, his brother was the athlete in the family.

The street is mostly deserted this time of day, and I have my gun out and up and am running with it like it's a relay-race baton. Sprinting like this, the trick is to never put my finger inside the trigger guard, not until I mean to shoot. And I'm not going to take a wild shot, not unless I have to, not unless he gets close enough to the Rue de Maur that I have no other choice.

I close on him now like a wolf after a rabbit, and he takes a mad right around a corner, leaping in front of a pair of Vespas, causing their drivers to brake, lose control, and slide out on the pavement.

I follow behind, hurdling the lead bike like a goddamn Olympic athlete while maintaining my speed. I don't know these streets that well, certainly not as well as Luis, but I'm pretty sure he's going to have to take a left to cut into the Rue De Maur if he's going to have a chance at reaching Coulfret's building. I duck to the lefthand side of the street like a sheepdog guiding his charges into a pen, and Luis makes a mistake, the biggest mistake a man can make when he's being pursued by someone who wants to kill him.

He looks over his shoulder.

There are two reasons this is a bad idea. The most obvious is that he is no longer watching where he is going, no longer looking at the sidewalk in front of him, and any slight crack in the pavement could send him sprawling.

The second and equally devastating reason is the man being chased gains a glimpse of how much ground his pursuer has made up, spots the look of conquest on his enemy's face, realizes the hopelessness of his goal. It's enough to sap the energy out of even the fittest of men.

Luis takes one quick look over his shoulder and I see his eyes go wide, his adam's apple bob, and a look of panic spread across his face. Like I mentioned with his brother, panic can cause two things.

He stutter-steps, giving up precious ground, stumbles a bit, throws his arms out to gain his balance, and is successful enough to keep moving forward.

But the panic gave me all I need. I overtake him in a dead run, and raise the gun when I'm a foot away. One step, two steps more, and I fire close, right into the back of his head.

He drops like a stone, and I only stop long enough to snatch up one thing from where it fell on the pavement before I'm up and running again. I don't know if anyone is following me.

I'm not going to look over my shoulder.

CHAPTER FOURTEEN

RUBY LIES ON MY BED WITH HER EYES SHUT.

"Don't say it."

"Say what?"

"Just don't."

"I wasn't going to say a word."

"You get him?"

"Yeah. And his phone. I tossed both his and his brother's into the Seine."

Ruby nods, expressionless.

"But I'm uneasy about the computers in his apartment. I couldn't risk going back there, and once the police look into the dead bodies, they're going to find—"

"Don't worry about it." She hasn't opened her eyes. And now that I move around the bed, I see she's dressed the knife wound with the kit from my bag.

"Why shouldn't I worry?"

"I took care of it."

"How?"

"I threw all their computer shit into the fireplace and lit it up."

"With a knife sticking out of your arm?"

"Nah, I yanked it out before you got out of the building. Used your shirt to tie it off, like you said."

She opens one eye to take me in, see if I remain shirtless. I'm wearing an oversized hoodie I found in a souvenir shop three blocks from where I overtook Luis. Even at close range, I avoided getting his blood on me, and raised no eyebrows in the store.

Ruby closes that eye again. I move to the bathroom sink and splash water on my face. It hits me at once, the weight of it, the near miss of having my face out there, the near miss of Coulfret knowing exactly who is gunning for him, and another pair of dead brothers who dipped their toes in a dangerous world, got caught in the maelstrom, and drowned. I don't know how long I stand at the sink with the water running. Seconds could be minutes could be hours.

"You know how you told me you were thinking about quitting the business?"

"Yeah."

"Well, I got something to admit to you."

"Oh-kay. . . ."

"Fuck it if you don't want to hear it."

"I'm listening."

That eye opens again to gauge my face, to see if I'm mocking her. Satisfied, she resumes. "When I banged through the door on his floor, all of a sudden, he was in the doorway, looking at that gun in my hand. And I don't know what to say but I flinched."

"Well, hell, that's nothing. It happens to all of us." Not true, but it felt like the right thing to say.

"Jesus, it's not that. I don't give a shit about that. I mean, I would've liked *not* to have flinched, because that's what allowed the frog to bury his knife in my arm, and caused me to miss, so yeah, I'm not happy, but no, that's not what I'm spilling my guts about."

She waits to see if I'm going to interrupt, but I keep my mouth tight. Her voice falls quiet, like the words are coming from a place deep inside her.

"When he got the knife in me and I dropped my gun and went down ... well ... I was scared. Not a little bit scared, mind you. I was *terrified*. It was probably only a few seconds, but it seemed like the clock stopped and the only thing I was thinking was 'please don't let him go for my gun.' My mind was telling my body to fight, claw, scratch, but it was like there was a complete and total disconnect and I couldn't move.

"I've never felt that before. I thought I was going to die here in Paris in some crappy apartment building and no one would ever know why or who I was or what I was doing. I'd just be a Jane Doe or whatever the hell they call it here. I was really, bone-deep scared. 'Please don't go for that gun, please don't do it. . . .' That's all I could think."

Her eyes are wide now, searching my face. I open my mouth, but she interrupts before I can speak. "Goddammit, Columbus . . . lie to me. That's what I need to hear right now. Just lie to me."

I start to speak again, but decide against arguing. Instead, I give her what she wants.

"Everyone gets scared," I say without a hint of conviction.

She turns her eyes to the ceiling and looks at nothing, her face tightening. The lie stays in the air a long time.

The train is cramped and crowded and smells like life. It is a good way to hide in plain sight or to lose oneself in the dark recesses of the mind. People shuffle on and off like ocean waves, constant, unaware of the sameness in their differences. I can ride for an hour without looking up, without moving from my seat.

Fear like the fear Ruby experienced is a costly motivator. It causes one to make ill-conceived choices, give in to irrational decisions. It can cause a person to overplay his advantage, like Noel's wounded driver trying to steer into me, or it can cause paralysis, a complete abdication of thought and function, like Ruby on the Mallery stairwell. And once fear takes hold of a person, it nests, laying eggs and defending its territory with sharpened claws. It becomes a drug, a fix, something the host thinks is necessary in order to perform. It's the opposite, though . . . hollow, a false high, a placebo.

I was going to use Ruby to lure him out, play off of that one nugget I found in the police reports. Get to him through his nose. Use what I'd learned from Risina regarding the rare-book world and apply it to the rare-wine world. Get her to pretend to be a high-end merchant, offer him a wine he couldn't refuse, a taste of a 1921 Petrus, and be there when he accepted the invitation.

But Ruby Grant's career will end soon. She'll slip or she'll panic or she'll step back when she should be moving forward. Fear is nesting inside her now, whether she knows it or not. The bluster, the swagger . . . that was the act. Maybe she'll have the foresight to walk away, to get out of the game early, before her ticket gets punched. But more likely, someone will take advantage of a simple mistake and put her down.

I won't be around to see it.

I need to move quickly. The dead Mallery brothers are probably on slabs at the morgue, and it won't take long for someone in Coulfret's organization to tip him. Once he learns one of his killers, Llanos, died in the city, immediately followed by the slaying of one of his henchmen, he'll understand I've come looking for him. I have yet to draw a bead on the third assassin, Svoboda, but there's no doubt in my mind he's somewhere close by, circling.

I need to lure Coulfret out of that apartment building on the Rue de Maur tomorrow, before he has a chance to bury in like a tick and wait out my demise.

I'm still going to get to him through his nose. And as much as I'd like to do this on my own, I'm going to need help.

"You want to be my fence, we start now."

Archibald's voice comes through the pay-phone line. "I thought you might come around, Columbus. We tied to that string like I said."

"Yeah, yeah . . . we'll discuss structuring our deal and parameters and all of that as soon as I get back to the States. But right now, I need some assistance in Paris. I need a scrounger who can work on the fly. . . ."

"Say no more. I got a fella works outta London . . . I'll have him there on the first train in the morning—"

"It's gotta be tonight, and he's gonna have to pull some serious strings."

"Where you gonna be?"

"Hotel Balzac. Room 202."

"He'll be there in two hours. Name's Olmstead. Bald, glasses."

"Thanks."

"My pleasure, Columbus. See you when you see me."

Olmstead enters in the dead of night. He's as Archibald described: shaved head, thick square-framed glasses, but he's big for a scrounger, over six feet tall. For someone whose job it is to acquire things, often illegally, I was expecting a slight figure, a man who doesn't stand out on surveillance-camera footage.

As is so often the case in this world, there are no greetings between us as he moves to the small desk in the room, sits down, and opens a tiny notebook.

"Now what is it I can get for you, Columbus?"

"A water and power truck. A jumpsuit, the kind a city worker would wear."

He looks up. "You're in luck. The water service in Paris is moving from a private company back to a city-run municipality. It's in complete and total flux. This year is the transition and it's running as smoothly as cobblestone. Won't be a problem."

He's got a blue-collar accent, and scars on his knuckles speak to his resourcefulness.

"What else?"

"Doctor's masks."

"Okay."

"Mentholatum."

"Okay."

"And I need the truck filled with bags of manure."

He doesn't miss a beat. "Bovine? Horse? Organic compost?"

"The kind that smells the worst."

Ruby watches us from the bed, lugubriously. I don't have to tell her she's out.

"Okay, what else?"

"I'm going to need two nameless guys. . . . "

"Shooters?"

"No, wallpaper. Two men dressed in the same uniform as me, directing traffic, nodding at pedestrians, and running like hell as soon as I pull the trigger."

"That's gonna be expensive."

"I'll pay 'em whatever you think they're worth."

"What else?"

"That's it."

"I understand you need this in the morning."

"I want to be rolling by eleven."

"Then I'll meet you two blocks to the east, in front of the Parc de Monceau, at 11 A.M. tomorrow."

"I'll be there."

He closes his notebook, coughs into his fist, and leaves without saying good-bye.

When I look at Ruby, she simply rolls over and faces the wall.

Coulfret's men pay us no attention as we park a block north of his building. Our truck has the blue-and-white insignia of the city printed on its side, and it only takes a moment for me to pop out of the back and open the adjacent manhole cover.

As I mentioned, Paris has an extensive sewer system, historic enough to generate its own tourism business. It would provide a somewhat easy path to enter Coulfret's building from underground if that were my aim, but I'm wary of attacking there. Like the Webb brothers, his home turf is well guarded, he knows it better than anyone, and I have no intention of ending up in the bottom of an elevator shaft.

The two men Olmstead found are impassionate and more or less featureless. They toss me bag after bag of compost as soon as I descend into the cavern beneath the street. The size of the chamber is commodious; I barely have to stoop. It takes me a dozen trips back and forth, but soon I have all of my materials in the right location underneath the Rue de Maur. Directly above my head is the main sewer line running into Coulfret's apartment building.

We move the truck to the middle of his block, directly across from his front door, and the first of Coulfret's bodyguards approaches, a young man with an out-of-style bowler cap. My two hired pigeons and I have doctor's masks covering our noses and mouths, and we are in the middle of prying up another manhole cover.

Bowler Hat speaks in colloquial French with a thick nasal accent.

"Keep moving. You have no business here."

I try my best to respond in a passable Parisian accent. "We're having trouble with the sewer conversion."

"I don't give a whore's fuck if you are prying out golden piping beneath the street, you don't do it here. Pack up your truck and—"

"You'll have to take it up with the city—"

"I'm taking it up with you, you son of a—"

And then I see him instantly recoil as the stench hits him, his forearm flying up to cover his nose.

"My God. . . ."

Two of his fellow bodyguards spring up as their cohort flinches backward. The nearest one, a bald mustachioed thug I recognize from the whore's pictorial spread, clamps his hand inside his jacket and raises his voice. "What is it, Anton?"

"Shit!"

"What?"

"It's shit. These sons of whores smell worse than a monkey cage."

The two approaching bodyguards now catch a whiff and reel backward. "Gadddd. . . ." I hear one of them grunt.

"I told you we were having problems. You didn't want to listen."

"Yes, yes, Jesus. For the love of the virgin, please, just cover that goddamn hole and drive away."

In a ruse like this—what is essentially a short con—if you play it right, the mark will believe it is his idea to give you what you want.

I nod at Bowler Hat, then turn to my men. "Okay, cover it, boys. They don't want our help, they don't want our help. I'm sure they'll have an easy time rescheduling with the city."

My pigeons start to recover the manhole when the first of Coulfret's inner circle steps out of the apartment building, waving his hands in the air, gagging.

"What the fuck?" he chokes out in our general direction.

"What is it, Philippe?" Bowler Hat shouts back at him.

"The toilets are flowing backward with shit!"

"Inside?"

"Yes, inside, goddamn. Where do you think I just came from?" A couple more of Coulfret's inside dwellers emerge like bomb victims from the house, sucking in huge gulps of air as soon as they make it to the sidewalk. Their disgust is coming out in angry cries directed at Bowler Hat, just for his proximity to us. He yells back defensively in a high-pitched voice that sounds like it is pouring directly from his nose. "I didn't do a fucking thing. I'm trying to get to the understanding of this!" He turns back to me, eyes red and teary.

"Fix it, you stinking whore. Fix it or so help me, I'll rip off your face and flush you down the sewer myself."

He then rips the doctor's mask off my face, snapping the elastic band, and holds it up over his own mouth and nose, daring me to complain.

"Okay, okay, no problem." I whistle at my guys to get back to work. "I'm really sorry."

"You should be sorry, you enormous shit bag."

He's taken a few steps back, and I pretend to watch my men work on the manhole cover, but my eyes are locked on the front door of Coulfret's building as more of his men emerge.

I'm scanning for anyone who looks like he's had plastic surgery on his face. I know Coulfret's height and weight and build and I've seen three pictures of him from before he faked his death, and I'm certain I'll spot him when he clears that front door. If he fancies himself a wine connoisseur, then there's no way he had any work done on his bird-like beak. I'm willing to bet he changed his eyes and his hair and his chin and his jawline but not that aquiline nose with the bridge that looks like an architect sculpted a flying buttress. I'll know it when I see it, and I'll put a bullet right through it and jump in the truck and get the hell out of here.

Two new men emerge from the front door, though neither can be Coulfret. One is too young and the other a foot short, and the din they raise as each comes out of the house hurling curses at the sky sounds like a demonic choir. One more thug trickles out, but he's far too skinny, and then I hear Bowler Hat yell at someone over my shoulder.

"Gerard! Is this the kind of shit we can expect from the city taking over? Shit, shit everywhere?"

I don't have to look over my shoulder to know who he's summoning; I understand from the first "ha ha" I hear bellowed back. The obsequious detective from the Bastille district who happens to be writing a novel about French crime approaches behind me, the same one who left me alone with the files on Coulfret.

Not now. Not right now.

Another two heavies lumber out of the building, but neither is

Coulfret and he's gotta come out any second and I don't need much but I need that now. The way to him is through his nose, and there just isn't any conceivable way he can hold out much. . . .

"Ha ha! Anton, it seems the stench of your sinful life is finally catching up to you, yes? Ha ha!"

The fat detective sweeps past me, biting into an apple, and I turn just enough to give him my profile, and for some reason he seems immune to the smell and he's happy to set up shop two feet from me, chomping on that apple like he's about to sit down for a picnic.

Three more men flood out of the door, one holding a handkerchief over his face, covering his mouth and nose. Is he Coulfret? He's the right size, the right body shape. But I can't tell with half his face obscured.

"Is this really bothering you, Anton? I would think a pig like you would be right at home in a den of filth."

I inch closer to the front door, toward the man holding the kerchief, waiting for him to lower it, please lower it, and there's something familiar about his eyes, but I can't be sure. Lower the kerchief, just give me half of a second to look. . . .

"Why don't you do something about it, you miserable goat?"

"I am doing something, Anton. I am out enjoying a nice walk in the neighborhood I love to serve, keeping an eye out for any unusual business, and do you know what I've been wondering?"

"I don't give a damn what—"

"I've been wondering why Roger Mallery and his brother were murdered in separate places last night."

Another two goons step out into the sun and join the man with the kerchief, and they are both too large to be Coulfret, but their body language indicates a deference to the man they've joined. If he'll just lower that fucking handkerchief and let me catch a glimpse of his nose. . . .

"What is this you say to me? What of Roger Mallery?"

"Dead on the roof of a building on the Left Bank, and the same night his brother is murdered on a street two blocks from here. But you know nothing of course, ha ha. You are just a know-nothing imbecile. . . ."

I'm riveted by the man holding the kerchief to his face and I can tell the exact pattern on it, a yellow and white floral stitch, and I can tell exactly how it folds back at the top into a little triangle, and I am imploring him, willing him with my eyes to lower it. Detective Gerard and the goon with the bowler hat pay me no attention, an arm's length away, as my pigeons stoop over the manhole cover like they're actually working, trying to find a leak in some subsurface piping. I have to hand it to Archibald's scrounger, he found unflappable men and whatever he's charging for them, I'm going to double it as soon as we get out of here.

"I'm up to my ears in shit here and you want to question me like I'm down at your stinking police station?"

"Why is your face turning red, Anton? Is it because the story I heard is true about you having an incident with Roger Mallery concerning some thuggery you did together near the river Seine?"

"Do you think, you cow, maybe my face is red because the street smells like a toilet and now the building behind me is stinking to heaven and this miserable ass is gawking when he should be working."

The man with the kerchief is just lowering it as I realize Bowler

Hat is talking about me. And there it is, that unmistakable hook nose, and yes, the shape of his face has changed, and yes his eyes have changed, but that nose remains the exact bulging mar to his face I first examined in his mug-shots. The man is Alexander Coulfret, the one who put the price tag on my head for accidentally causing his brother's death, I'm sure of it.

I can feel Detective Gerard turning in my direction. I block him out, keep my eyes on my target as I drop one hand behind my back and return it fisting my Glock.

"Mr. Walker?" I hear Gerard say, confused.

I turn my eyes just enough to see Bowler Hat hesitate, his brain working out that I am raising a gun and he is going to be too slow to stop me.

The manhole cover clanks down hard on the ground as my two pigeons recognize the moment is at hand and sprint away like track stars.

Surprise is slipping quickly, and a professional killer knows the wise move is to close the distance to the mark as efficiently as possible. I abandon all pretense, break character, and charge Coulfret, arm raised stiff.

He spots me coming and is smarter than his men, puts it all together in an instant, how I flushed him out and am now moving in to finish the job.

A threatened animal's instinct is to break for home, shelter, security, the place he feels safest, and Coulfret does the same, spinning on a dime and darting back for his front door.

Gunshots break out around me as the bald mustachioed heavy or maybe Bowler Hat or any of a half-dozen thugs I'm ignoring try to squeeze a shot off at me, but I remain focused on the prize and pull the trigger and a puff of red mist explodes as I wing Coulfret just as he bursts through his door.

There is nothing I can do but follow.

CHAPTER FIFTEEN

THE STENCH IS A BEING, ALL-ENCOMPASSING, A PHYSI-CAL PRESENCE, AS POWERFUL AS A KICK TO THE STOM-ACH. Despite my precautions—I rubbed mentholatum under each nostril, the way coroners do when dealing with corpses—the manure trapped in the building has successfully battered my defenses. All I can do is push it to the side of my brain, treat it like a wound, like pain, and ignore it as best I can.

I thought Coulfret might have mounted an assault as soon as I barreled through the door, but only a blood trail leads down the corridor to my left. Instinctively, I spin around and double-bolt the door. He turned this building into a fortress, which I can use to my advantage to keep his men at bay. If there are other ways inside, I hope this at least buys me enough time to finish my work and somehow escape.

The blood streaks on the concrete floor are more splashes than drops, and though I didn't see exactly where I hit him, it had to have been more than a glancing blow. He's not going to last long without medical attention, and maybe not even then. My first thought is to take my chances and concentrate on getting the hell out of here, but I have to know this is over, know Coulfret is dead, know the contract has been lifted. If I don't see it with my own eyes, if I don't finish him, I'll always be looking over my shoulder. This has to end now.

I hear pounding on the door behind me, big angry blows like someone is trying to put his foot right through the steel, but the locks are holding as I continue to stalk down the hall. It'll take them some time to break it down, but I don't know how much. I don't know if it'll be enough. The red streaks become even more prominent on the tile, more defined as I follow them, picking up my pace.

The blood trail ends at the closed doors of the elevator.

Stairs. There has to be a stairwell nearby. I know he went down to the basement, the place he's most comfortable, and if he thinks I'm going to walk into the elevator car and wait for the drop, then the blood loss is affecting his head.

I fumble with a door nearby, nothing, then a second gives way, and I'm in the stairwell. I slow my breathing and deaden my footfalls as I soft-step down the stairs. I may be exactly where I don't want to be—in the mouth of the monster—but his wounds even the playing field and I am going to see this through now or die in his basement like all the others.

He wanted to send me a message, but I have a message to send back, one that reaches beyond these walls to the world within a world where I have my flag planted. My message is this: if you put paper on me, if yours is the signature on the contract, if you pay a hit man to hunt and kill the assassin known as Columbus, then you're signing your own death certificate.

I kick open the basement door, hoping the explosion of sound will draw a shot, but no volleys come my way. The blood trail is thicker now, large splashes of crimson leading from the elevator to the end of the hallway. The smell of shit pervades every pore in my skin. My eyes fog up, and I do my best to blink away tears.

The blood streaks end in a foot-wide puddle-and lying next to the mess is the body of Alexander Coulfret. He has stopped just outside a door marked simply "24," and I know it is the room he grew up in, the one he lived in for so many years.

And this is how you die in our business. Not gloriously, not surrounded by your loved ones, not in a peaceful bed with a priest giving you your final communion. No, you die on the street with your throat punctured by a stiletto blade. You die humiliated in the bathroom of a fishing-supply store. You die on a rooftop flopping forward, caught in mid-stride. You die on the stinking floor of a stinking basement just a few feet from where you first learned to walk.

Coulfret's body shudders. He is not dead, not yet. A cough starts from somewhere deep inside his chest and comes out as a gasp. He rolls over as slow as a glacier and turns so I can see his face. Blood covers his lips and I'm reminded of the whore who took the pictures, the one with the lipstick smeared across her teeth. His complexion is the same as hers, and any color he once had is in full retreat. It turns out my bullet found the side of his neck, and he can no longer raise his hand to cover the wound; he's too weak to even try to keep the blood inside.

I'm shocked he made it this far, lived this long with a wound that severe. It's a testament to Coulfret's strength, an additional volume chronicling his force of will. And yet it's also cause for alarm. When the mortally wounded live this long, it's usually because they have something left they want to say, some unfinished business they wish to complete. Coulfret still breathes because he has a message to send me.

"You're Columbus," he croaks out, spraying blood when he hits the last syllable.

I don't answer, and his eyes are only focused in my general direction.

Another coughing fit racks his body, and it takes me a moment to realize he's not coughing. The bastard is laughing. It's an unnerving sound, a devil's chortle.

With every bit of his strength, he pounds out his last words. "You think killing me frees you?"

His eyes shift again, this time to the door to his father's apartment. For a second, I think he is finished, but he has three words left to say.

"The contract pays."

Footsteps pound the stairwell at the same time as the elevator dings. Coulfret's men have finally knocked down the front door and infiltrated the building and, despite the smell, seem determined to check on the boss's health and then hunt me down.

Before the men fill the basement like roaches, I kick open the door marked "24" and disappear inside the janitor's apartment, Coulfret's childhood home.

The contract pays. The fucking contract pays. The goddamn fucking contract pays and all this was for naught. I am under it now, choking on it, swimming through shit of my own creation, and it will be impossible for me not to drown.

He must have set up some sort of trust where the contract pays out to the first man who returns with my scalp. That's what he wanted to tell me, what he wanted me to know before his eyes glazed over. I am Sisyphus with his rock, Tantalus with his grapes, and despite the fact I took the stairs, the elevator still collapsed thirty feet with me inside. I thought there was a chance out of this life with Risina, but that image is a mirage, a cruel trick of the mind. I am never going to break the water's surface, never going to breathe clean air. Even in death, Alexander Coulfret has made sure of that.

A contract killer has a bullet with my name on it, but not these men and not today. Their footsteps are a stampede outside the door as they congregate around Coulfret's dead body. In a moment, they'll be coming through this door and every door in the building, trying to find me.

Inside Coulfret's kitchen, covered by a throw rug, I find what I'm looking for: an old-style floor drain. I pull the manhole cover tool from my pocket and pop the metal grate, then ready the heel of my boot to knock the copper pipe away. One, two, three kicks and it falls back, hanging limply like a broken arm. I drop through the floor into the sewer, just as the door to Coulfret's apartment flies open.

I have half of a minute head start. I hope it'll be enough.

The sewers are pitch-dark, but there is a pinpoint of light fivehundred meters away and I realize it's from the manhole cover on the neighboring block, the place the pigeons and I first unloaded the manure. We must not have put it back all the way, a mistake I don't usually make, but occasionally a mistake can be a savior.

Since I'd spent a great portion of the morning in these sewers, I'm slightly familiar with them, another advantage I should have over my pursuers. I know to run at a crouch to avoid overhead piping, and I know the walkway near the walls is relatively flat and so I set out as quickly as I can toward that sliver of light.

It grows sharper, more pronounced as I approach and grip the steel ladder leading up to freedom. I hear voices, amplified off the stone but still far away, screaming about grabbing a flashlight, screaming about the smell, screaming about my escape.

"So this is Italy? Kinda what I thought. Old buildings and old people."

We're in Siena, a small town an hour outside Florence. It's quiet and confined and a bit isolated, and we sit in the tiny dugout basement of a traditional restaurant. There's only one stairwell descending to this level, and I sit facing it.

Archibald Grant has flown in for the occasion, namely to mollify his newest partner. He looks up from where he's picking at a bowl of pasta, wipes his mouth with his napkin, then clears his throat.

"So this french fry put paper on you and told you after you popped him that it pays no matter what?"

"That's it."

"Yeah . . . I've heard about something like this before. It's rare and it's tricky, but there's a way around it."

"I'm listening."

"This Cole-Frett . . . he got family?"

"All dead."

"Wife, spouse, nieces, nephews?"

"No."

"Loyalists in the organization?"

"I don't know. I know of one I heard about. A guy who helped him with his original coup. Martin Feller."

Archibald writes the name down in another one of those coil-wire notebooks.

A shuffle by the stairs draws our attention and Ruby descends into the room, smiling. Even with her arm in a sling, she has her bounce back. As she takes a seat at the table, Archibald flashes her his grin.

"What's shakin', baby girl?"

"Ready to eat a goddamn burger at Blackie's."

"I hear that. I been out of the country for all of twenty-four hours, and already I feel a bit wobbly. Why the fuck can't they cook up a regular burger and fries here, man?"

I just shrug.

"Goddamn. Okay, anyway, what'd you hear about fallout from Paris, Ruby?"

"The organization's in complete disarray. That whole neighborhood's locked down tighter than Leavenworth. Not only did you kill the boss . . . a French cop was killed there too. Shot down in the street just outside the building."

This is news to me. I wonder if Detective Gerard tried to interfere or, just as likely, caught a stray bullet intended for me. I liked that fat man; listening to him on the street talking to Bowler Hat, I realized the chatty, dim personality was an act, a weapon to uncover whatever he was trying to dig up. Underestimating him was my mistake, but I guess it doesn't matter now. If he suspected I was anything more than the writer I pretended to be—the more I think about it, the more likely it must be—well, I guess that suspicion died with him.

Archibald breaks my reverie, still addressing his sister. "You know who filled the power vacuum?"

Ruby shakes her head. "No, but I get the strong sense Coulfret wasn't all that well liked by his men."

Archibald turns to me. "Okay, you see? This might not be as desperate as it seems. He may have extended the contract even after he's down in a box, but he still has to have someone physically pay out the transaction. Could be his lawyer, could be a fence . . . or could be this Feller you mentioned. Whoever it is . . . that's the person we need to negotiate with. Not the way you do it, with that Glock of yours. The way I do it . . ."

Ruby finishes his sentence. ". . . with that silver tongue."

"You know it."

"I'm not much on sitting and waiting. I've been running around with paper on me for too long and I have to admit, I don't like the feeling."

"Give me three days. I'll hit Paris and shake the bushes."

"And me?" Ruby asks.

"Bite into a burger at Blackie's."

"Say no more. I'm out of here." She stands, smiling again. Any residual effects of what she told me about her fear of dying seem to be forgotten. She is her old cavalier self, and if it's an act, like Detective Gerard's dummy bit, it's a good one. Maybe I was wrong. Maybe she'll come through this after all. She certainly doesn't seem bitter that I excluded her from storming Coulfret's building on the Rue de Maur. She wouldn't have been much help with that bum arm anyway.

I stand, and she looks disappointed when I offer her only my hand.

"I'll see you back in the forty-eight, Columbus."

"Yeah. Thanks for everything."

"Don't mention it."

She heads across the room and ascends the stairs.

As soon as she's out of earshot, Archibald whispers conspiratorially. "What d'ya think?"

"Of Ruby?"

"Yeah, of Ruby. Who the fuck else would I be talking about?"

"I like her."

"You think she's gonna make it as a professional?"

I keep my voice even, walking the line between telling him what he wants to hear and what he doesn't. "How the hell should I know? She worked through some tight spots— "

Archibald holds up his palms and stands. "Say no more."

Maybe I should try to placate him, reassure him about his sister. Maybe I should voice my concerns, let him know about the fear I saw gripping her back in Paris. Maybe I should say a lot of things, but I can't seem to muster the energy.

"All right, then, three days."

"I'll be here."

The circle in Siena contains a single tower that sticks up from its center like a middle finger. I stand at the top of it, staring out over the town and the neighboring Tuscan countryside. I feel at once both exposed and safe, a paradox that is somehow comforting. This is the place I reside, straddling the line between vulnerability and security. It is the world I have lived in for as long as I can remember. If my fate is to spend the rest of my life hunted, I won't do it in the shadows: I'll stand at the top of the tower and dare the bastards to come.

And I'll do it alone.

The wind picks up and chases gray clouds across a gray sky. The horizon seems close and blurred at the edges, claustrophobic. Only a smattering of pedestrians are on the sidewalks below, grouped in twos and threes. The wind provides the only sound, a low whistle like a dirge.

More than anything, the aftermath of this mission has made one truth clear: the next time I see Risina will have to be the last. She deserves better than me, better than what I can give her.

A knock at the door and Archibald enters, flashing his broadest smile, though this one's not part of his act. He's genuinely happy with himself.

"What'd I tell you, Columbus?"

"What'd you tell me?"

"I said to let me take care of it. So I took care of it."

"Come on. Get to it."

"All right, all right. Here's the straight word. The killer I told ya 'bout what calls himself Svoboda? He's still after you, and he's not gonna stop till he's dead or you're dead."

That sounds like nothing to smile about, but before I can say anything, Archibald keeps going. "Something to do with the kill fee being promised already and no one wanting to deal with the ramifications of canceling on the motherfucker. But . . . and here's the big but . . . come to find out a lot of people are glad Cole-Frett is ten toes up and six feet under.

"Power vacuums don't take long to fill, no matter what language you speak. The name you gave me, the one who was loyal to him? Feller?"

Archibald draws his finger across his throat. "Dead. Found bobbing up and down in the river they got there with his wrists cut and bled out. Authorities called it a suicide, but you and I know better than that. These boys want to wipe their hands clean of all things Cole-Frett. They sure don't want to pay no more kill fees. As far as they're concerned, you did them a favor. What's done is done and bygones be bygones and let's sweep it all under the rug. They got enough to deal with concerning the dead cop. If Svoboda winds up plugged, more power to ya is the message they gave me."

I nod, digesting the information. "So then Svoboda and that's it?"

"You get him before he gets you, slate's clean."

"So let's get him."

"How you want to handle it?"

"Turn the boat around and meet him head-on."

Archibald smirks and points his finger at me. "I like the way you think."

"You gotta dig deep, Archibald. I want the file to end all files on this guy. I want to know anything and everything about him."

"Ain't gonna be a walk in the park. I'm pretty good in the States, but over here's like walkin' around with my hands tied behind my back."

"Do whatever you can, and do it quickly."

"All right, Columbus. Where you want me to be?"

I say it without thinking. "Rome. Piazza Navona. One week."

He looks at me long and hard, but I keep my face unreadable. If he knows I have a girl there, he's keeping the information to himself.

Finally, he nods. "I'll be there."

When I approach my motorcycle, Ruby is waiting for me. "I haven't left yet."

"I noticed."

She looks like she has something she wants to get off her chest. She rubs her fingers over her knuckles, then takes a long breath.

"I got about twenty minutes before I head to Florence. Listen, I just thought I'd—"

"You don't have to say anything."

"I do, though. I do. So let me do this." She looks down at her feet and toes the pavement rubble. There's no hint of pretense in her voice, only earnestness. "It's that . . . when you told me before that you were thinking about getting out of the game, I know you meant it."

"Nahhh. Like I said, I was just yammering. Forget I brought it up."

"No, you weren't. You saw something in me that told you it was okay to drop all the barricades we build around ourselves. You showed me your real face."

"Maybe. I don't know. . . ."

"It's why I trusted you enough to tell you about me, my first time. I like the bond we share, Columbus. It's a hell of a lonely job."

I nod, knowing she has more.

"So, who is she?"

My throat starts to constrict and I cough into my fist, just . . . what? Attempting to hide from the truth? Am I that conspicuous? That easy to read?

"What d'you mean?"

"There's a girl out there who has you thinking of ditching this life, checking out of this world."

Something inside me that I thought was further from the surface rears its head. "Yeah, there's someone . . ."

"Well, then, here's what I'm trying to say, so I'll just say it. This girl wherever she is, whoever she is. . . ."

"I know. I know. You don't have to tell me. I need to. . . ."

"You need to go to her and leave this game and never look back."

I guess surprise registers on my face, because Ruby pounces on it like a cat.

"I told you I read your file. I've read a lot of files on a lot of hired killers. And the one thing they all have in common is that they have nothing and nobody and no reason to leave this gig. Every one of them is alone. They're all like condemned prisoners waiting for the executioner to lead them to the noose. I'm included in that. I thought that made me better, somehow above it, like I was a wolf standing on a mountain looking down at the sheep. But you know what I finally figured out? The people, the civilians . . . they're the ones with the power. They're living, man. Really living. We're just the ghosts they pass in the street."

Her voice is filled with emotion, raw and electric, like a lightning storm.

"So you go to her, Columbus. You got a chance to shake off these chains and live. If you don't take it, you're a fool."

It takes a moment for me to realize she's finished. My ears ring, her words chasing away the fog. The fear I pinpointed in her is equally rooted in me, but only now do I realize the depth of it. It's not a fear of dying anonymously, of dying painfully. The fear is that

I'll die without having lived. Without really having lived.

When I speak, it's little more than a whisper.

"And if the life catches up to me? Or her?"

"Outrun it, Columbus. Make 'em think you're already dead."

For the first time, maybe for the first *real* time, I can see it. Not a mirage, not a vaporizing dream, but a tangible, reachable image. I can take a cue from Coulfret, get our names on a list of dead travelers and disappear. Vanish to a place in the country, a place away from the trappings of the professional life. A place devoid of contracts and violence and death.

And why did Ruby tell me this? Does she see a strength in me she doesn't possess herself? Does she want to walk away but can't get her feet to move? Or is it because she hasn't found someone to walk away with?

"You got a suitcase somewhere you need for your flight?"

"Nah. Archie takes care of all that."

"Then hop on. I'll give you a ride to the Florence airport."

"I got a car coming . . . should be here any minute."

"We'll cancel it."

"Is this your way of kissing off my advice?"

"It's my way of saying thank you."

She half-grins and rolls her eyes. Maybe she believes me and maybe she doesn't.

I step off the bike to fetch her the spare helmet I keep underneath the seat when a bullet whizzes by my head and hits Ruby square in the face. Her forehead caves and her body falls like the earth reached up and yanked her down.

For a split second I think I should just stay here, just let it happen, let Svoboda take me out too. I could step off the plank, walk into the quicksand, let *this* be my escape. Not fake my death . . . hell, make it real, make it count.

And just as quickly, instinct kicks in and I am diving and wheeling in the direction the bullet came and another shot rips the ground next to my head and I scramble away from where Ruby fell, keeping low, another shot explodes closer and I slither my way to the relative safety of a bus bench.

I can't stay here, though, stay in one place. I have to keep moving, fend him off before he gains position on me. I take a quick peek but can't find anything to target, and if he's expecting me to break for my motorcycle or try to help Ruby, then he should have shot her somewhere besides the bridge of her nose. She's beyond needing help; Ruby was dead before her body touched the ground.

I discharge a full clip, including the bullet I have racked in the chamber, and then break for the alleyway to my left, dropping my clip and re-racking while on a dead sprint.

A fourth bullet ricochets off a stone edifice within an inch of my ear and please don't let this be a dead end and please get me through the next two minutes so I can pay this goddamn bastard back.

I run hunched over, trying to make myself smaller, providing the narrowest possible target, and the alley funnels out to a cobblestone street. I feign left and break right and as soon as I'm clear of the alley, I slam on the brakes and press my back into the wall.

I don't want to think, not now, not about Ruby pleading with me to get out of this life, to escape it in a way she knew she couldn't, and her face disintegrated by a bullet intended for me. Shut it down, block it out, bite it back, and focus.

A half a second to scan the alley and he's there, at the opposite end, a thin man with simian arms and dark features clutching a pair of pistols and I swing out and we squeeze triggers at the same time, two ships steering into each other.

A bullet kicks up gravel behind me, and I see Svoboda whirl around and maybe I clipped him, but I'm not sure. He disappears around the entrance, the way he came in, and if he's playing possum then I'm going to run headlong into his ruse. I sprint up the alley, and there's no sign of blood, and I hear an engine catch and roar, and when I peek around the side, my motorcycle shoots away.

I look down at the rubble. Ruby lies where she fell, a dark halo congealing around her head.

This is how you die. Faceless and, before long, forgotten.

Not any more. Not Ruby. A car is pulling to the curb, a black Audi, the driver Archie had ordered to carry his sister to the Florence airport.

A plump man opens the door and steps out, looks around, wiping sleep from his eyes, and then spies Ruby's body on the pavement.

"My God," he says in Italian, and the next thing he hears is his car screeching away behind him.

I've been on the wrong end of the hunt for far too long and it's past time to flip the switch. Svoboda's running now, and that means I must have wounded him. Maybe just a nick, but enough to toss him off his plans, and if there's an advantage I can wring out of this sorry mess, then I plan to make the most of it.

I duck my chin and blitz through the gears, redlining the tachometer, as up ahead the motorcycle takes a corner without slowing, Svoboda's knee practically scraping the street. He slingshots out and up at a ninety-degree angle, managing the corner without forfeiting speed. He can handle a bike better than I can, damn him.

I sweep into the same turn, throwing up the parking brake as I downshift and slide out. The Audi drifts into the turn and careens off a parked Smart Car before straightening again. I'm on his tail, but he's got six blocks on me and I'm not sure if the Audi's got the engine to catch a motorcycle.

Svoboda doesn't give me the chance.

He swings the bike around like it's on a turntable, points it in my direction and throttles the engine. Before I'm sure what's happening, an avalanche of bullets peppers my windshield, shattering the glass. I only have a half second to duck as this madman, this medieval fucking jouster, unloads an entire clip into my interior. The seat behind me explodes like a hand-grenade went off, and I jerk the wheel involuntarily as I bury my head in the floorboard.

The car lurches to the left like a horse stumbling out of the gate and smashes into God knows what and whatever advantage I had is gone. I hear the motorcycles engine buzzing past somewhere out on the street, or maybe that's just my ears ringing.

He's better than me. This realization bangs around inside my head like a bullet. *This son-of-a-bitch is actually better at this than I am. He turned the tables on me before I knew what was coming, went from defense to offense in the blink of an eye, rope-a-doped me like a three-dollar stooge on amateur night at the county fair.*

I have to make a move now or it's over, and, goddammit, I will not let it be over. Not hiding in the floorboard of a fucking car in Siena while he drops the bike, walks up, and shoots me through the empty windshield. Not while Ruby lies dead in the street. My engine is still running; I can hear the Audi's purr even as my ears try to pick up the sound of approaching footsteps.

Without poking my head up, I throw the car into reverse and slam the palm of my hand on top of the accelerator, pushing it down flat. The car responds, lurching backward and just when it gets up to speed, it slams into something else and I knock my shoulder into the dashboard, but if there's ever going to be a time for a peek, this is it. I pop my head up like a gopher coming out of its hole, and quickly look left and right.

Gunfire flashes in front of me, forty yards down the street, but the bullets whiz harmlessly over my head, and I see my backward maneuver surprised him. He has to change out his clip and now it's my turn to grab momentum.

I throw the car into drive, spin the wheel, and race at him while he's reloading. Even while I close the distance, he sits on his bike, *my* bike, in the middle of the road like a goddam matador. Fuck, I thought I was calm under duress but this guy sure as hell doesn't rattle.

I realize my car isn't going to get to him before he has his ammunition locked in place and clearly he's thinking the same thing . . . I'm delivering myself right to him.

At the last possible moment, I open the driver's door and dive out, abandoning the car to complete the mission for me. I hit the pavement hard and roll up onto a knee.

The motorcycle is roaring away, out in front of the car, easily evading it as the Audi starts to lose momentum and slowly comes to a stop without actually crashing into anything, weak and ineffectual. I stay on the sidewalk a long time, but he never comes back.

CHAPTER SIXTEEN

THE END IS RARELY FINAL. IT IS INGRAINED IN US FROM BIRTH: THE END OF A DAY LEADS TO TOMORROW; THE END OF WINTER LEADS TO SPRING; THE END OF A YEAR BEGETS A NEWBORN, PALE AND INNOCENT AND VULNER-ABLE. The notion permeates our literature and culture: the end of a phoenix gives way to a new bird; the end of a king signals the coronation of his offspring; the end of a savior leads to a miraculous resurrection.

It is this singular idea, perhaps more than any other, that there *are* no endings, that there is *always* another sun coming up, another day dawning, a life beyond this life that keeps the machinery of the earth turning. The peasants toil in the fields, the workers grind for their paychecks, the solders sacrifice in battle in the hope that the end is rarely final, that they will have given of themselves so that others will continue on in a somehow changed world.

And what if the end *is* just the end? What if once you're caught on the hook and pulled into the boat, and you flop around on the deck before breathing your last breath, what if the world never knew you existed, what if you did nothing to benefit this place, what if it is just the same as it was before you came? What if the end is rarely the end, but it is for you and you're the one erased?

Or what if when you close your eyes, when your heart stops and your neurons quit firing, what if in that moment, the world simply ceases to be?

The sun sits high in the cloudless sky, alone, imperious. The heat is oppressive, like it's coming both down from the sky and up from the street. Pedestrians move around languidly, like there are weights tied to their ankles. Ladies fan themselves with magazines in a futile attempt to push air away from them, but the heat clings like ticks. Dogs lie in the meager shade of shop doorways, tongues out, panting. It is a hell of a May day in Rome.

Five of them have passed since Ruby died in Siena, and Italian police are looking for two men fleeing the scene, one on a motorcycle and one in a stolen black Audi. Details are sketchy; no one got a good look at the killers so early in the morning.

I spent the last five days on the coast, sitting in a hotel room, staring at the gray ocean, clearing my mind. I'm pissed about the motorcycle; that bike had treated me well. The only treasure of mine

Svoboda can puzzle over is a first-edition copy of *The Compleat Angler*, which I'm sure he'll find in my saddlebag. Maybe he's flipping through it now. I purchased another copy, a paperback edition, from an English-language bookstore named Feltrinelli in Florence before I fled for the coast. In the five days prior to arriving in Rome, I read the book through twice.

Archibald waits at a tiny table, eyes covered by dark glasses, dressed in black. His expression is as sober and grave as a funeral director's. The first thing I notice is how gaunt his face looks when his smile is gone. When I take my seat across from him, his fingers stop drumming the table.

"I'm sorry," I tell him.

"When I told you before I didn't have any uncles or aunts or relatives I gave a fuck about, I was lying."

"I know."

"She was there— " he stops, like he's having a hard time getting his mouth around the words. He steadies himself, then takes another stab. "She was there every moment I needed her, every inch of the way."

"I know."

"Was he gunning for her, or did she catch one intended for you?"

"I have no idea."

"Why didn't she leave when I told her she was off? Why'd she stick around?"

"She wanted to tell me something."

He levels his eyes in my direction. They spill over with pain. "What?"

"She told me I should quit the business. Disappear."

"Now why the fuck would she tell you that?"

"She knew I have a woman waiting for me."

He takes that in, and, like when he let me in on the secret that he had a sister, he knows I didn't release that information lightly.

"Tied on that same string, Columbus."

"Yeah."

It is true. There is no use denying it. Archibald Grant and I will forever be tied on that same string. A man who goes by Svoboda made sure of that on a quiet street in Siena.

Archibald slides a file to me underneath the table. I place it in my lap and the same weight hits me, the same heaviness I felt when William Ryan handed me a similar file with Jiri Dolezal's name at the top of the page. When will it be too much? When will the stack of rocks on my chest finally overcome me?

"I haven't slept in five days," Archibald says. "Save a nod here or a wink there. Everything I got, I put into that file."

"Okay."

"I visited Doriot in a Belgian prison. He turned me on to three other European fences. I've been to Madrid, Prague, and Munich. I got tongues to loosen and I got memories to be recalled. Every bit of knowledge about Svoboda is found in those pages. The only one who knows more about him is the Lord Almighty."

"You know this makes you a target as well. He'll find out you've been sniffing around his background."

"Let him come."

I nod. "Well, thank you. You did well."

Archibald stands like he's going to leave, then drops his hands in his pockets. He suddenly looks old, like twenty years have passed since I saw him in that subterranean restaurant in Siena.

"Drop him, Columbus. Drop him and then get the hell out like Ruby said. I'll make sure no one comes for you."

For a moment, he stands there, a ghost, like these words sucked out the last bit of his energy, like it's not me who has been crushed by the stones, but him. Then he turns and disappears into the crowd.

I open the file. Tomas Petr Kolar grew up an only child in eastern Czechoslovakia, in a village named Krasnik, long before the country split into two. His father, Petr, was an avid hunter when he wasn't serving the party in the factories, assembling railroad machine parts to be shipped to Poland. By the age of four, Petr had taught his son how to take apart and reassemble a VZ-24 rifle. Together, they shot wild hares and pheasants and roe deer and the occasional mouflon in the hills surrounding their village.

Kolar's mother was diagnosed with lung cancer when he was eight years old. He and his father watched her wither away until her face looked like a tight sheet stretched across a skull. She died fourteen weeks after her diagnosis, in a hospital bed, mumbling gibberish.

For two weeks, his father ignored him. For two weeks, he made his own bed, fixed his own dinner, bathed himself, and cleaned the house while his father sat in a chair staring out the window.

At the end of those fourteen days, his father shot himself in the head with the VZ-24 rifle. The man was thirty-eight years old. There is no indication Kolar was there when his old man placed the gun between his knees and pulled the trigger. But no one can say for sure.

There is a large gap of knowledge in the file from that point. No one knows where Kolar was taken after his father's suicide, where he was raised, where he received his education, who trained him in the art of assassination, when he changed his name to Svoboda. Archibald speculates he was in the military, but wasn't able to confirm it. However, Svoboda's early work involved the use of a CZ-2000 short assault rifle, a rarity left over from the Czech army's special forces missions behind NATO lines in the late nineties. He also carried a CZ-100 handgun, another weapon first introduced to the Czech army in 1995. It's convincing evidence the boy was scooped up in the military machine soon after his father's suicide. Maybe he bunked with another soldier named Svoboda and assumed his identity after the man fell in battle? Any guesses would just be speculation, but I'll pocket the name Tomas Kolar. Knowing it could very well come in handy.

The first true knowledge of Svoboda's whereabouts as an adult came in March 1999. He completed two contract killings that month, five days apart. One in Prague, one in Amsterdam. The assignments were distributed by two different fences. Two completely unique, unrelated targets.

This information is staggering. Two jobs within five days? Putting aside the psychological ramifications, this act teeters on recklessness, if not outright insanity. How could he plan his hit, or, even more importantly, his escape? How could he be sure he'd get to his target and get away with the kill?

I flip through the file just counting up the hits Archibald was able to uncover. From the three fences plus Doriot, Svoboda has averaged fourteen kills a year for the last half-dozen years. Fourteen! More than one a month. And that's just the ones Archibald found out about.

I flip further and focus in on one kill Archibald coaxed out of the Spanish fence. The assignment was to eliminate another professional contract killer, a British hit man named Ogle. The two came together in a hotel corridor in Carlisle, in northern England. For some reason, both men lost their guns and ended up fighting hand to hand. Svoboda gained leverage and bit into the larger man's neck, severing his carotid artery and ripping it out with his teeth. All while hanging on to his back like a lion taking down an elephant.

I flip through dozens of hits for which Archibald was able to carve out a few details, and an interesting story emerges. At least ten of his kills involve contracts on other assassins, maybe more. It seems he's developed a niche for himself, a specialty, an area where there appears to be steady work. It seems Svoboda has forged a business out of hunting hunters.

I study these closely, the hits specific to taking down men like me. Nearly all of these kills involve close, contact murder, without weaponry. Strangulation, choking, biting, beating, eye-gouging, cracking necks. This must be intentional. He doesn't want to shoot these men from a distance; he wants to destroy them with his hands. If I can figure out why, maybe I can crack the code on how to defeat him.

Another one of his kills leaps out at me. In 2006, he was hired to eliminate a French hit man named Garrigus. The hit took place at an apartment in Toulouse, a hideaway belonging to the French assassin's mistress. When the two bodies were discovered, the police made note that the girl was most likely killed first, by a bullet wound to the back of the head, before Garrigus drowned to death in the apartment's bathtub, his hands restrained behind him with plastic ties.

In one other instance, Svoboda killed a woman along with the mark. Again, she was killed first, by gunshot, and then he disposed of the target with his hands, choking the man to death behind a pub in London. That's all the information Archibald collected on the kill, but it speaks volumes.

Svoboda is more than a professional hit man. He may be very good at what he does, he may be a top earner, he may never default on a job, but he is no Silver Bear. He's a goddamn serial killer. He doesn't care about the contracts, the hunt, the getaway, the strategy, the creation of a connection that can be severed. He gets off on the actual killing.

Svoboda and I are nothing alike. We may have the same job, but we perform it in two different worlds. I thought he was better at this business than me, but now I know that simply isn't true. He might have skills and courage, but the skills are reckless and the courage is fueled by some sort of tortured madness. He can be beaten. I'm sure of it.

I devour the file, reading it and re-reading it until I have every page memorized. Archibald has outdone himself again. The file is as thorough as any I've been given. And all the information leads to one conclusion: Tomas Petr Kolar, also known as Svoboda, wants to work in close so he can kill me with his bare hands.

I think I'll let him try.

I know the question before it is asked. Why would I go see her? Why am I so heartless, so depraved, so selfish, that I would put her in harm's way, at this moment, when a killer who lusts for blood is hunting me, has already killed in front of me? A killer who I know likes to rack up as many bodies as possible, who actually thrives on leaving a mess?

She is in the middle of a sale when I enter Zodelli on the Via Poli. Risina's face lights up as soon as she spots me, her cheeks flushing with blood. If it's possible, she's grown even more radiant since I last saw her, like the recent sunny days have knocked out the underlying sadness and brought her beauty right to the surface.

I take a seat in a stuffed leather chair and watch her work.

". . . a five-volume first edition we will only sell as a set. It contains 367 hand-colored folio lithographs, all produced by Joseph Wolf, who was the leading ornithological artist at the time. You see? Gould personally selected him. Beautiful."

The man she is speaking with is the size of a bear and has a thick Russian accent. "Remind me about the binding?"

"Of course. Contemporary full green levant morocco, with elaborate decorated spines . . . yes? Marvelous. They contain raised bands, marbled endpapers, and as you can see, all the edges are gilt."

"The price is still one-fifty euro?"

"Yes, Mr. Bembatov."

"Hmmph. Thank you."

He turns, measures me for a moment, then shuffles toward the door like one of those old weeble-wobbles, like his weight needs to list side to side before it can move forward.

The bell above the door is still jingling when she crosses the room and is in my lap, in my arms.

"One-fifty?" I say, eyebrows raised.

"Thousand. It is one of the finest book sets we own. This is the fourth time Mr. Bembatov has been in to look at the complete set. He asks the same questions each time. But I'm beginning to think he's a fish who won't bite."

"Oh, then I'll buy the set first. Would you like a credit card or . . . ?"

She slaps my chest playfully, then kisses my neck, my cheek, my head, my lips. Finally, she rests her forehead against mine.

"I don't like this, Jack. Not at all. I don't like it when you're away and I can't talk to you. I envision the worst. And if something were to happen to you, I would never know. No one would come tell me."

"I won't put you through this much longer."

"That sounds ominous."

"I didn't mean it to be. I told you I was looking to make a change."

She untangles herself from me and stands, a smile on her face. "I choose to still believe you. I do think you mean it."

"I do. I mean it."

Her face abruptly changes, like she just remembered something disheartening.

"I have some disappointing news. I'm sorry, I just thought of it . . ."

"Oh?"

"I consulted all over regarding your story, the one of the boy in the silver wagon. I even contacted three people in the United States who specialize in children's literature. But no one has knowledge of this book."

I nod, and for some inexplicable reason, this saddens me. I guess it shows on my face.

"I'm sorry. I don't know who else to contact. . . ."

"Forget it. Like I said, I'm not sure where I read it. For all I know, someone may have made it up and told it to me as a child. I spent some time in some rough places. Maybe somebody told me the story as a form of escape. I don't know why, but it stuck with me."

"If you had the author's name or knew one of the character's names. . . ."

"I wish I did. I just . . . don't."

She looks chagrined.

"Honestly, don't worry about it."

She nods, and then her face brightens, like she's glad the bad news is out of the way. "How long will you be in Rome?"

"For a while. Let's have dinner tonight."

"Yes! Where should we go?"

"Do you know a place that is quiet, dark? A place where no tourists go?"

"Yes, a block from my building. A restaurant with four tables. It is called Dar Filettaro a Santa Barbara. Should I write that down?"

I laugh. "No, I can remember it."

"I'm off work at six. Please tell me you'll be there at six fifteen."

"I'll be there at six fifteen."

"I missed you, Jack."

"I missed you too, Risina. More than you realize."

He can be beaten, I tell myself on the way out the door. *I'm sure of it.*

She is dressed in a soft green gown, the color of mint leaves, and her hair is up, tied in the back, so her shoulders are exposed. I notice a freckle there I hadn't noticed before, and I think *there is still so much to discover.*

"You must order the fried baccala. It is their specialty. The best in Italy."

"I will. Thank you for the recommendation."

I have my back to the wall in the corner, and a glance over Risina's shoulder gives me an unobstructed view of the door. We are the only ones in the restaurant at this hour.

She leans forward, a glass of wine in her hand flirting with the candlelight.

"You told me that when you returned, Jack, you'd tell me your story. You'd tell me everything."

"I plan to."

"I won't force it out of you."

"I will tell you. But not yet. I need a few days to arrange some things. Then I promise I'll lay everything out for you."

"Ahhh. . . ."

"You should know . . . my story . . . it's not pretty. It's not tidy."

"The best stories are rarely symmetrical."

"I'm not sure you'll like it."

"I wish you wouldn't make a judgment as to what I will or won't like."

"Fair enough. Let's just say I'm not sure my story has a happy ending."

She grimaces and, for a moment, doesn't reply. I have a feeling there have been very few happy endings for Risina. "Does this mean you'll be leaving Rome again?"

My eyes don't leave her face, but she senses my hesitation. She leans back, takes a sip of the wine.

"Never mind. It doesn't matter. Let's enjoy your time here."

"Risina. . . ."

"I told you I would not judge you, Jack. I won't."

The waiter emerges from the kitchen and takes our order and Risina looks down at the table. If she is biting back emotion, she won't show it to me.

He can be beaten, I think again. *I know I can beat him.*

"The arrangements I have to make . . . are for both of us."

"What do you mean?"

"This is going to come across . . . truth is, I don't know how this is going to come across." I stop, chewing over what I want to say before plowing forward. "What I do . . . I was serious when I said I don't want to do it any more. I want to escape it. I want to get out and never look back.

"My father . . . I know this is coming out of left field . . . but my father thought there was only one way out for him. I'm sure it seemed like an easy way out, but it never is. For a long time, I believed that route was the way for me too. But since I met you, Risina . . . since I met you, my thinking changed. I want to escape and live. I *choose* to escape. But I don't want to do it alone. I want to escape with you."

Before she can respond, I press on, locking my eyes on hers. "I have money, enough money so neither of us would ever have to work again. We can live on a beach somewhere. Or the woods if you prefer it. Or a farm. Or a hut in Africa for all I care. I know it's not fair to ask, I know you barely know me, but I know this is right. Maybe for the first time in my life, I know what is right."

She hesitates, making sure I am finished, and in that moment's hesitation, I think I've lost. I played my cards, my best hand, and I came up short. But then she utters one word packed with hope.

"When?"

"As soon as possible."

"And where would we go?"

"Wherever you want, as long as it's away. Away from congestion and traffic and people."

"And I would leave everything behind? Say no good-byes?"

"Yes."

"And we would be together?"

"Yes."

She looks up and her eyes shine, though no moisture spills out from the lids, no tears fall down her cheeks.

"Okay."

"Okay?"

"Yes. Okay." She reaches across the table and takes my hand. Hers is trembling. She is barely breathing.

"If after a week, a month, a year you decide this is no life for you, that I'm not the man you thought I was, I'll never stop you from returning. But I promise to you, Risina, I'll do my best to be the man you want me to be."

The food arrives, but after nudging it with her fork, she looks up at me. "Do you mind if we go to my apartment? Forget dinner and we just . . . you just hold me?"

I can beat him. I know I can. I can beat him.

"Let's go."

For three nights we meet after the bookstore closes, at various small restaurants near her apartment. For three nights, we leave without eating and lie in her bed, holding on to each other as if we are afraid to let go, afraid if we loosen our grip, the other will vanish like smoke. For three nights, we say very little. For three nights, we live, and breathe, and love.

On the fourth night, Svoboda comes.

CHAPTER SEVENTEEN

IF I WERE SVOBODA, HERE'S HOW I WOULD GET INSIDE. I WOULD SCOUT COLUMBUS BEFORE HE DISAPPEARS INTO THAT BASEMENT RESTAURANT IN SIENA, AND I WOULD WATCH AFTER HE LEAVES TO SEE WHO ELSE COMES OUT.

Then I would follow the black girl, the other assassin, out of the building to see where she is headed. I would watch her, excited, as she waits around town instead of leaving. I would instinctively know she wants to meet with my target once more, that she has some unfinished business she wants to get off her chest. I would read it all over her face.

When she makes contact with my mark, I would jump at the chance to shoot her from a distance. My goal is not just to kill my target, because where is the satisfaction, the inherent thrill in that? No, my real aim is to make my target suffer before I end his life. Before I make him look me in the eye while I destroy him with my hands.

I've done it before. I've killed those close to my mark. My contracts are supposed to be for men like me, but these men are nothing. They are weak. The first rule of being an assassin is that a professional hit man cannot afford relationships of any kind. These relationships can and will be exploited. It is the staple of our business: to hit the target where he or she is weakest.

So I have. I followed one to his mistress. I shot the whore first, causing my mark to lose his edge, to give in to anger, to come at me wildly. I used his rage against him, kept him off balance until I was able to force him down, force his hands behind his back, force his wrists into restraints. From there, I filled his bathtub with water and watched him drown a hundred miles away from any ocean.

So many of these men, these debasers of my profession, I've found to have chinks in their armor, found to have an affinity for the opposite sex. I've taken pleasure in proving to them just how foolish they are, how selfish, how infantile their decisions are to bring women into their lives. These men are not unlike my father, my stupid fool of a father, who couldn't see a life for himself after his own wife passed away. Who stared out a window for two weeks before blowing his head into the wall. How weak he was! How dumb!

How goddamn selfish and stupid and sad.

Imagine my surprise when this target, the one called Columbus, did not hesitate after I shot the black woman. How he immediately abandoned her. How he only cared for himself. I thought he might double back to help the woman, at least hesitate when her head exploded, but I was wrong.

Here, finally, is a formidable opponent. Here, finally, is a man like me, a Silver Bear, a man who puts his profession, his own life, first. I take his motorcycle and ride off with no helmet because I want to feel like him, to become Columbus. I turn and face him in the street like a gladiator, like a warrior, and only when I realize I have no more bullets, my reloaded clip is empty, do I retreat.

If I were Svoboda, in the hold of the motorcycle I would find a curious book, a four-centuries-old text by Izaak Walton titled *The Compleat Angler*. An ancient fucking book about fishing, of all goddamn things. Why this worthy opponent would choose this book, why he would leave an object like this behind, would be beyond me.

And then my fingers would alight on something maybe the owner didn't realize was there. Maybe the person from whom Columbus bought the rare book had tucked it in there without his knowledge, or maybe he had used it as a bookmark and forgotten about it. For inside the book, tucked between the last page and the cover, is a business card. It reads: Zodelli Rare Books, with an address on the Via Poli in Rome. And a name is printed underneath the embossed logo for the store: Risina Lorenzana, Chief Acquisitions Agent.

If I were Svoboda, I would flip the card over on the back and read Risina's home phone number, printed in black ink with a steady feminine hand.

If I were Svoboda, I would steer the motorcycle toward Rome. I would find this bookstore, locate this Risina Lorenzana, and wait.

I am sure Svoboda was disappointed to find that I, after all he'd heard and witnessed, was like so many of the others he had killed. That I had a relationship with a woman. That the black woman he shot in Siena was only an unfortunate associate while the real prize waited in Rome.

At the same time, I'm sure he was thrilled to have another chance to wound me, to make me suffer before he got his hands around my throat.

He must've been watching. Either that first night, or the second, or the third, he watched us meet at a public restaurant, and he watched us leave without eating, and he watched us walk the short distance to Risina's apartment. He marked the building and the window that lit up on the second floor shortly after we entered.

On the fourth night, he must've slipped inside her building and waited for us to come home.

I hold Risina's hand, her fingers locked in mine. We're feeling more comfortable now, like the idea has settled in and we're actually going to do this, going to just leave and not tell anyone where we're headed.

We've decided on a tropical location in a country where few people speak English. It's remote, but not so isolated it doesn't have Internet service, doesn't have a way for Risina to receive Italian-language books. I think her trepidation has given way to excitement, that what four days ago seemed so foreign now seems attainable.

We enter her building and head inside the elevator. It is barely large enough to fit both of us, and she leans into me as it rises, her back to my front. Her hair is right under my nose and it smells like cedar.

There have been no warning signs, no bad omens. I haven't lost my wallet or had coffee spilled in my lap or bumped my shin into a bench. We ate dinner without incident and talked warmly throughout the meal. And now we stand in the elevator, fitting together perfectly, two halves of the same circle, like we've done this all our lives.

She opens her apartment door, scoops up the mail, and moves to her sofa, taking a seat on one end, tucking her feet underneath her as she starts to sort through the envelopes.

"I need to use the bathroom," I say and head through a small door just off the main room.

There are three things I'm sure Svoboda doesn't know. One, I'm sure he doesn't know that I've marked the doors and windows with tape, similar to the way I marked my crawl space in Positano. If an outsider entered the apartment, I'd be able to tell in the first three seconds I'm in the room with just a casual sweep of my eyes.

Two, I'm sure he doesn't know that the bathroom I am moving toward has a second door, one that leads back around through the bedroom and enters the living room from the opposite side.

And three, I'm sure he didn't read *The Compleat Angler* carefully, if at all. Otherwise, he might have come across a passage in the fifth chapter. A passage I read over and over. A passage I memorized. It reads: "for you are to know that a dead worm is but a dead bait, and like to catch nothing, compared to a lively, quick stirring worm."

Risina looks up to see Svoboda coming at her with his gun out, his finger on the trigger. He has his free hand with his index finger covering his lips, signaling not to make a sound. On his face is a grim satisfaction, the look of a fisherman who first feels a tug on his line.

"Tomas Kolar!" I scream from his left, where he's not expecting me, and he stutters for just a moment, the surprise of that name and the surprise that I know it and the surprise of where I'm coming from all combine to provide a half second's hesitation. He pulls the trigger, just as I launch at him, and the shot goes off wildly, plugging into the opposite side of the sofa from where Risina is perched.

Now she does scream as I take him down to the floor and pound his gun hand into the wood, once, twice, and he gives it up, letting it go while swinging his elbow around in an attempt to shift the leverage.

I should've shot this fucker when I rounded the corner and saw him with his gun hand out and up but I couldn't be sure I'd force him to miss unless I took out his arm with my bare hands.

He wallops me in the cheek with that loose elbow, and this is the fighting in which Archibald's report said he excels, close-contact grappling, and again he smashes me in the ribs. Before I can get my hands around him, he sees an opening and flips me over onto my back and in seconds, I can feel his teeth breaking through the skin of my neck. He's a street fighter, a dirty fucking lunatic, and everything is fair game.

The smell of blood fills my nose, and I just have a second to think *my blood, goddammit,* and I'm going to have to do something drastic and do it quickly. I use all of my strength to buck up like a Brahma bull, flipping my entire body over and my defensive move does the trick, his teeth come off my neck and he slides across the wood toward the door, toward his gun.

Just as he reaches for it, Risina's boot kicks out, sending the pistol flying toward the bathroom, and both Svoboda and my eyes track it all the way till it comes to a stop equidistant from both of us. Our eyes lock once more and I can see him make the calculations instantly . . . can he get to the gun before I do?

Risina jumps away, pushing her back against the wall like she's trying to disappear through it. She holds her breath, watching, waiting.

Svoboda's expression turns to fire as he decides against going for the gun. Instead, he springs around and throws open the front door, fleeing, just like he did when his bullets ran out.

Without thinking, without looking at Risina, I leap after him, bursting into the hallway like a missile and I close the gap between us in what seems like seconds. There won't be a chance to regroup, a chance to play this tragic drama out on another stage. This ends here, tonight, and so help me God, it only ends one way.

He jumps inside the open elevator a half step before I do and turns to receive me and I plow into him with the full force of my weight, lowering my shoulder like a ram and hitting him square in the chest.

His back smashes into the wall of the car, but he absorbs the blow and tries to get his fingers into my eyes as we lock together in the three feet of space.

I shake my eyes free and am able to ball my fist and throw a blow directly into his stomach with everything I have. The air rushes out of his lungs and in that instant, I have him. My hands immediately clamp on to his throat like a vise, and no matter how much he thrashes, and how wildly he kicks, and how desperately he paws, I do not loosen my Beowulfian grip.

I can feel the elevator car descending as Svoboda continues to claw at my fingers, trying desperately to pry them off his throat. Maybe we bumped into the button during the initial impact or maybe someone below is waiting on the car, but my concentration on the task at hand doesn't flag. I am not going to let go and he knows it.

It won't take long now. I wonder what his final thoughts are as I watch his eyes begin to roll backward. Is he thinking it is fitting he's going to die not by gunshot, but with a man's fingers clasped around his throat? Is he thinking about all the times he's been on the other end of this situation, that he's been the one to kill a rival assassin with his bare hands? Is he thinking about where he must have gone wrong? Is he thinking about Risina, about how I used her as living bait?

If I were Svoboda, I know what I'd be thinking. I'd be thinking I shouldn't have taken this job.

Risina's face is as white as a gravestone when I enter her apartment. I was going to tell her everything. Maybe I should have done it sooner. Maybe it would have made a difference.

She crosses the room and has her arms around me and her face buried in my chest before I can react, squeezing with all her strength. I hold her as tightly as I can, losing myself in it, my mind blank.

When she finally loosens her grip and leans back, her face has regained its color. Her voice is strong, though there is a slight quiver in it.

"Is he . . . ?"

"Yes."

She nods. "I think we should leave now."

"Are you sure?"

"I'm sure."

Outside her apartment, Rome is at once both quiet and alive. We walk up the sidewalk in the general direction of the train station, my arm around her waist, leaving the body, leaving that life behind.

I wonder how soon Italy will call to Risina after we leave. I wonder if she'll find it difficult not to answer.

EPILOGUE

WE'VE COME TO LOOK FORWARD TO THE AFTERNOON
SHOWERS, WHEN GRAY CLOUDS GATHER OVER THE MOUN-
TAIN LIKE MISCHIEVOUS SCHOOLCHILDREN BEFORE HEAD-
ING DOWN THE HILL TO DROP BUCKETS ON OUR HEADS.
The air cools as the wind picks up, blanketing the village in a thick
sheet of mist. Then, just as quickly, the sun emerges as though from
a short nap, and chases the clouds out to sea. Shunned, abandoned,
they thin out and fade to nothing.

The only outsider I've talked to since coming here is Archibald,
once, soon after we arrived. I took a bus to a distant town and purchased a pre paid mobile phone.

"You gone, Columbus?"

"I'm gone."

"Good. Your tracks are covered. So stay gone." And he hung up.

I've had a few months since then to tell my story, and I've spooled it out for Risina slowly, afraid too many details about my life would lead to a conflagration, burning down the relationship before it had a chance to build. After the showers, when the beach is at its coolest, we lie in the sand, and she lets me talk. Usually, her knees are up by her chest, her arms wrapped around them, her eyes focused on mine. She nods encouragement when I hesitate, or asks for clarification when I leave out details, or presses me to repeat something if I recount it too quickly. Never once does she flinch, though I can sometimes see grief in her eyes.

I tell her of my mother, and Abe Mann. Of Pooley and Mr. Cox. Of Vespucci and the man who called himself Hap Blowenfeld. I tell her of two men named Ponts and Gorti, of a bookmaker named Levien, and a girl I once loved named Jake Owens. I tell her of all my assignments, all my jobs, all my fences, from Vespucci to Ponts to William Ryan to Archibald Grant. I tell her of Anton Noel, of Leary, of Llanos, of Svoboda. Finally, I tell her of Ruby.

She asks me about the end, the incident in her apartment. I explain to her about getting inside my target's head, about trying to see the world as he sees it. That I have used this technique throughout my killing career as a psychological mechanism, that once I am inside my target's head, connected to him, then I can sever the connection and continue to do what I do. I tell her how I applied that to Svoboda, that by being his target, he became mine.

When I discovered that Svoboda on several occasions killed the girlfriend, mistress, lover, or wife of his targets, I knew the best play was to use Risina as bait. To settle into a routine, meeting her after work each night, going to dinner in a conspicuous restaurant, retiring to her apartment, until Svoboda picked up on the pattern and attempted to exploit it. From Archibald's file, I knew I was better than him. That I could beat him. I *knew* it.

When he stole the motorcycle and had the book, I knew it wouldn't take long for him to find her. I couldn't leave until he did. If we ran, he would follow. So while he stalked, I planned the trap. Dangled the living bait, let it wiggle in front of him, and then pulled the line when he struck.

Risina takes this information the same way she's taken everything I've told her: as stoically as Epictetus. I don't know if I was expecting her to get angry, abusive, maybe to slap me for admitting I used her as bait, but she does none of these. Instead, she closes the distance between us and presses her lips to mine. When night comes, we cross the beach to our home and go to bed without eating. Sometime in the night, I hear the shower going. How long she's been in there, I have no idea.

She appears in the doorway, her hair wet, swept back from her forehead, framing her face. She is naked, and with the moonlight snaking through the window, her body is exposed, vulnerable.

"I know your name isn't Columbus," she says softly, swallowing, gathering her strength. "And I know it isn't Jack Walker. You didn't know me when you met me, and I realize now you would have never given me your name. I understand . . . I realize I don't know your name, your real name."

She folds her arms across her body. Her eyes never lower, never leave my face.

"So what I want to know . . . what I have to know . . . what is your name?"

And I tell her.